HER BILLIONAIRE
COWBOY'S
Second Chance

HER BILLIONAIRE COWBOY'S *Second Chance*

GALLOWAY SONS FARM
A FAIR CREEK ROMANCE
BOOK 1

CATHY SHOUSE

Her Billionaire Cowboy's Second Chance
Galloway Sons Farm
A Fair Creek Romance Book 1

Cathy Shouse

Interior design and formatting by:

www.emtippettsbookdesigns.com

Chapter 1

Sierra Delaney squinted out of the front picture window of Delaney's Diner and sighed. The American flags waving from the light poles along Fair Creek's Main Street lifted her spirits but offered no solution to the scrape she'd gotten herself into.

Just a few days from the Fourth of July, and she'd made headlines. Not the good kind, either. She picked up the *Gazette* and mumbled aloud, "Wyatt Galloway is a Clothes Stallion since he dresses so far ahead of the regular clothes horses." She tossed the paper onto the counter of Delaney's.

"You okay?" Annie York, her cousin and employee, handed over a food-and-drink ticket.

Sierra took the ticket and inhaled. "Something I wrote, my way of venting, really. It got published in the letters to the editor by mistake."

Annie leaned in and whispered, "What was it?"

At least I can understand whispering now. She'd recently broken down and gotten hearing aids for the first time, since she hadn't heard well for a few years.

"See for yourself."

Her cousin plucked the ticket away from her and picked up the newspaper, then headed back to the grill. "Somebody's got to get this food started."

Sierra glanced over toward a cluster of men huddled over coffee at their usual table. The mid-morning sunlight beamed on their mostly salt-and-pepper haired heads. No one's cup was empty that she could tell. She appreciated regular customers, and they added an air of hominess as they shared jokes and more serious concerns alike. If only there were more like them. Lots more.

She could relate that a couple of them had hearing aids, and found it no big deal. Not at all.

I'm only thirty-four, though.

She had started wearing them last week, but everything seemed distorted. She moved away from the refrigerator, its motor sounding like a big truck hauling corn at harvest time.

Lord, why do I have to deal with hearing problems, on top of everything else?

Annie returned with the food order in a bag, which she set on the counter, then spread out the *Gazette* and read, "The last thing Fair Creek needs is a fancy cowboy." She looked up. "This isn't like you. I mean, we tease a little, and this isn't a huge deal. Not really. But what were you thinking?"

"I read an advice columnist say that to get someone out of your mind, you should write a letter to them and don't send it." She gestured toward the paper. "Skip to the middle."

While Annie finished, Sierra fluffed the tendrils of hair left outside of her ponytail, to make sure they hid the brown plastic in her ears. She shuddered inwardly.

She'd gone in wanting invisible hearing aids and came out with bigger ones because she needed amplifying speakers. She wanted to keep a low profile about them until she adjusted. If it weren't for the health department guidelines about hair and food servers, she'd abandon the ponytail and really hide them. Who needed the double-takes when somebody noticed for the first time, or when they exaggerated how they spoke by talking extra slow and loud—even if they did mean well?

A bell over the entrance jangled. Annie frowned as she read. "What?" She looked up, with fire in her eyes. "How could you call Wyatt Galloway a Clothes Stallion? Seriously? It's weird for me because I'm dating Caleb Galloway. What if he asks me about it?"

"I wouldn't want to complicate your relationship with Caleb and I'm sorry. Galloways wouldn't read the paper. You're probably safe. But how did this happen?"

Annie nodded. "That's what I'd like to know."

"Mommy!" Annie's eight-year-old daughter bounded into the diner and wrapped her arms around her. The child had been at a friend's house.

"Hi, 'Aunt' Sierra."

Her heart warmed at hearing "aunt." "Hi there, are you hungry?"

Chloe's head bobbed up and down. "What are you guys arguing about?"

Annie gave Sierra a look that conveyed with her eyes to follow her lead. "Nothing, honey."

The little girl put her hands on her hips. "I'm not a baby. Who called who a horse?"

Sierra leaned down to her height. "I've left chocolate chip cookies in the kitchen for you and get a carton of milk out of the fridge."

"Yippee!" She scampered off.

Annie folded the newspaper. "This is signed by Anonymous. Who's going to know it's you?" She tucked the *Gazette* in to recycle. "Besides, the Galloways are more laid back than I used to think."

"You would know."

Annie's pale complexion turned pink. The two of them shared similar skin tones but Annie was blonde haired and blue eyed as compared with Sierra's red hair and hazel eyes. "It's hard to believe Caleb and I've been dating since Christmas." Wyatt Galloway's younger brother, Caleb, had visited in December and became guardian to twins. Annie had fallen for the babies and their uncle wasn't far behind.

"You've all been through quite a lot."

Her cousin's blue eyes took on a pained expression and she nodded. Silent moments passed between them. "In some ways, losing his dad has brought us closer. It's deepened our faith."

"Then some good has come out of heartache. Seems to me you're meant to be together."

Annie's eyes took on a dreamy look. "You think so?"

"I do, and Chloe will be happy, too. But you better wipe that look off or the guys'll call you Goo-Goo eyes again."

"I don't like it when people talk about me."

Sierra grinned. "That's the price of living in Fair Creek."

Annie straightened up. "Now if we can just find somebody for you. It's not healthy to have your whole life tied up in Delaney's."

"I've got enough just trying to keep this place from sinking. I sure hope you're right that no one will read that letter."

Someone waving a coffee cup caught her eye. Ted Mitchell, whose wife had died three months ago, wanted her attention just as Chloe came back from the kitchen.

"Be back in a minute."

She refilled Ted's cup first and moved around the table. "You've been here a while. Have you achieved world peace yet?"

"We saved that for tomorrow," Ted said. The men chuckled. "Today we're hashing out the problems with solar panels. That Wyatt Galloway comes from a good family, but we're opposed to his company."

She'd done enough already on the subject of Wyatt. "Well, as always, thanks for coming in."

Wyatt's picture had been in the *Gazette* a lot due to the public meetings and controversies of solar energy in the next town over. They'd been best friends in school and hadn't seen each other since. His photo in last week's paper had reminded her of old hurts. That had to be the reason she'd written that dopey letter. *Apparently, I've gone back into high school mode.*

Annie and Chloe were refilling the straw dispensers at the counter, neither of them smiling. Chloe's eyes looked a bit red like she'd been crying.

The little girl's lip quivered. "Aunt Sierra, it's all my fault." She swallowed and paused.

Sierra glanced at Annie, who just stood there, and didn't seem to know what to say. Sierra couldn't handle Chloe trembling and biting her lip, so she put her hand on her shoulder. "Sweetie, there must be a mistake. Why don't you tell me what happened?"

Short arms came around Sierra's waist. "I was playing school in your office. The papers on your desk were supposed to be my students' homework and I put them in a folder. I'm really sorry."

Sierra gave her an extra squeeze. "Oh, honey, it was a mistake. Thank you for telling me. I forgive you."

Annie clarified that Chloe had put papers into Sierra's ad folder, including her letter she'd meant only for venting. She'd unknowingly submitted the folder to the newspaper when she turned in her ad.

"That doesn't explain why Alice published it."

Annie shrugged and sent Chloe back to watch TV in the office. Annie's phone pinged indicating a text message.

She read it. "Hey, I know it's a pain but could you make the food run out to Galloway Sons Farm for me? Caleb needs me to watch Ella and Drew. I could put them in their playpen and tend the diner, too, while you're gone. Chloe would help."

No. Just no. But as if Annie sensed Sierra's reluctance, she doubled down on her request.

"Pretty please?"

After John Galloway died in January, the sons were making their way back to the family farm, helping how they could. Sierra didn't want to run into Wyatt. They hadn't parted on good terms and she *really* didn't want to see him since her letter had gotten published, on the off chance he would have seen it.

"Wouldn't it be simpler if you went out to the farm and watched the babies there?"

"Trust me, I lobbied for that last night." Annie yawned. "I was up all hours to do a *major* cleaning for Caleb to come over, not easy once Chloe had gone to bed. But Caleb's got business in town and I wanted to help however I could."

Annie's messiness was a source of friction between the couple. "I can't understand why your place is such a disaster. If you'd take the time to pick up after yourself, have a place for everything, and get Chloe on board, you'd see a world of difference."

"Not everybody was born organized. Thanks for the tips." She seemed anything but grateful. Regret lodged like a knot in Sierra's stomach. Staying out of these conversations had always worked best for them.

Calm yourself. Sierra needed to stop running like a scared rabbit. Wyatt was rarely around the farm. And so what if he was?

She was an adult and would handle it.

"Oh, okay. That's not a problem." Sure it wasn't.

Chapter 2

Sierra drove along the road to Galloway Farm, taking in the deep green of the cornfields under skies that were multiple shades of blue. Cattle were catching some shade under a tree, their tails flicking away flies, which took her back to spending time on her grandparents' farm.

Exceptionally large, fluffy clouds, like gigantic cotton balls, stretched as far as the eye could see. Passing through the big wooden arch with Galloway Sons Farm in bold letters above the lane brought home how it dwarfed her grandparents' property. A tractor pulling a wagon with two men bailing hay brought back Grandpa tackling those tasks, into his 70s. He tended cattle while she and her cousins played in a wooded area near the creek and searched for tadpoles. One summer they had to bottle feed a newborn calf that had been rejected by its mother. The cooking sessions with grandma had meant everything to her.

She entered the house without knocking, as always. Male voices drifted out from a back area where they were washing up, a routine she was familiar with from catering there in the past. She couldn't be sure whether any Galloway sons were home, but she thought their vehicles were missing. Making herself at home in the big old kitchen with oak cabinets that matched the wood trim, the sun streamed in through sparkling-clean windows. She smiled, humming as she plugged in the slow cooker with the chicken and noodles. On autopilot, she prepped the mashed potatoes, rolls and green beans with bacon crumbles. The huge commercial stove had been set to preheat before she arrived, and she placed most of the food inside to warm up.

She reached to bring the beans out, and her knuckle grazed the inside of the stove. Ouch. She rinsed her hand under cool water for several seconds.

When the men filed in to the table, there were no Galloway faces, and relief made her legs weak and her concentration improved. If they met, she didn't want to put him on the defensive. What could he really say about lack of communication? Her efforts to write to him or call had failed. He'd left and not looked back. Sadness from that time weighed on her and it was out of proportion, given what a long time ago it happened. Her challenges, with the restaurant, and her hearing, were making her long for a simpler time. Maybe that was it.

Soon, she was serving the pies. She packed up her things and planned to wash up her serving dishes at home, leaving any leftovers in their refrigerator.

The important thing was to act like she didn't care now. She realized how much she wanted to be out of there.

What if Caleb decided he needed Annie to go with him and the twins? But that wasn't the real reason she was on edge. The longer she stayed, the more chance of Wyatt coming in.

Finally, she was ready to leave and could feel a clean getaway on the horizon.

A few minutes later, in the outdoors, she covered the ground quickly, loaded down with everything in bags and holding onto the multiple handles to make one trip. At the barn where she'd left the van, she catapulted toward the back doors that folded out for easy loading. Coming closer, the doors of the van were cracked open, not latched shut.

She must have been preoccupied with thinking about that letter to the editor when she arrived. Sierra reached the doors, opened them wider. Setting her armload down on the edge and scooting everything in further, sunlight poured in and illuminated the space up near the cab. From deep inside, a pair of glittering eyes peered at her. The world's biggest raccoon squatted near the back of the cargo space, crouched over. He held some type of food in his paws.

"Eeek!" Her high-pitched shriek even scared her.

Rocky Racoon looked up in surprise. The black markings around his eyes made him look menacing. The animal gnawed on bread she'd meant to take inside. It stretched up to its full height and fixed his beady little eyes on her. She leapt back, heart pounding, and landed smack against something solid.

Someone with serious muscle mass.

She wanted to see who it was but the beast chose that moment to walk forward, holding her full attention. The furry thing with pointy claws suddenly vaulted past spiders on her greatest-fears list.

Firm hands landed on her hips. "Whoa there. Easy does it." A man's calm, steady voice came from somewhere above her head. *Thank you, Lord.* But she couldn't move and her hands trembled.

His arms slipped loosely around her waist, and she detected taut muscles even through the sleeves of his suit jacket as he eased her backward. Sierra made her feet follow.

Whoever it was had a woodsy scent and he loosened his grip as they moved together. "Give him space to leave. He's more scared of you than you are of him."

"I seriously doubt that. Who studies raccoons' brain patterns, anyway?"

He snorted. "Just go with it, okay?"

Shaking, she tried to catch her breath and slow down her heartbeat. The animal trudged to the van's edge and dropped its bulky body down to the ground, lumbered away and disappeared under a bush by the side of the next barn over.

A black-and-white dog with markings like a Border Collie, only larger, bounded up from the field and pounced in front of her like he wanted to play.

The dog's pink tongue hung out and its brown eyes sparkled. The man's voice said, "You missed the action, Bentley." He cocked his head at the sound, then ran to the bush where the racoon had disappeared. "Woof! Woof! Woof!"

"Bentley, no. That's enough." The dog took off back where he'd come from. Sierra turned and gazed into deep brown eyes under a cowboy hat with a fringe of dark hair that spilled onto his forehead. He was still the most handsome man she'd ever seen, his jaw line as sharp as ever. The shoulders were broader than when she'd seen him last, and his long legs even longer. Her chest ached, for whatever reason. It really was good to see him. The cowboy hat managed to complement his business suit with an expensive cut, tailored to fit his lean body. His Western-styled boots were polished, without a speck of dust on them and reminded her of how she'd admired his feet when they used to spend summers swimming in the creek and going barefoot everywhere.

What was wrong with her?

The name escaped from her lips in a whoosh. "Wyatt Galloway."

She frowned, pinning him with her gaze, and trying to focus her thoughts. "You snuck up on me."

With one eyebrow raised, he looked at her like she was a rattlesnake about to strike. His voice came out gruff. "I warned you I was coming up from behind."

He *did*? Heat flushed her face. Hearing aids didn't bring your hearing to perfect like glasses could match 20/20 vision. She shrugged. "Guess my mind was somewhere else. You scared me."

He raised a brow. "You're blaming *me*, instead of that critter?"

Why should she explain that with her back toward him, unable to detect his lips moving, she'd missed his call out to her? He'd never explained anything to her ever. Nothing at all. "I wouldn't put it past you. You always did know how to make an entrance."

Stepping away, he tilted his head, and the sun revealed the stubble along his chin. Something registered deep down that she hadn't felt in a long time, maybe ever. She wondered what those whiskers would feel like under her fingers. Sierra swallowed.

Wyatt's assessing gaze locked with hers. He'd been able to read her well back in the day, when they'd been best friends. He held out his arms. "Do you need a hug?"

They'd said that a lot, mostly as a joke, but had always followed through. She'd forgotten until now. Startled by how much she wanted to, she hugged him lightly, leaving major distance between them, basically giving him an air hug. His voice rumbled above her head, sounding just fine with her hearing aid amplifying it. "That old coon did a number on you. But I *have* just flown in, am jet lagged, and could use a shower." He paused. "Scary stuff."

"I'm quaking in my boots."

Thank goodness he didn't know what seeing him again was doing to her insides. She managed to step away before things got more awkward.

She had liked their friendship partly because of how unaware he was of his own charms. "You flew in from Indy? You don't look rumpled at all."

Not that he had ever been anything but perfect in appearance when she knew him.

He lifted his hat exposing dark, close-cropped hair except for the curls gone haywire along his forehead. He replaced the Stetson. Her mouth went dry. Seemed a shame to hide hair that gorgeous, just like everything else about him.

"First decision we made when we lost Dad was to upgrade the air strip he registered as an airport years ago on the back acreage. Private jets save time."

Must be nice to have money. Not that it stopped the hurt of losing parents.

Tears pricked in back of her eyes. She'd lost Mom at age 15. His mom had been gone a few years. "Please accept my sympathy about losing your dad. I'm so sorry."

Wyatt nodded and sadness came into his eyes and his mouth turned down. "Thanks. We'd gotten our relationship to a better place so I'm grateful for that."

A motorcycle out on the road roared by and he turned toward it, the sound clearing Sierra's head. For all these years, she'd imagined what it would be like to run into him. Of course, it hadn't entered her mind she'd be shaking from a raccoon encounter.

Or that good memories would flood in with the not-so-good.

"Remember my motorcycle, we used to ride through town, you behind me."

"Yeah, I do. Aunt Lucy was always pestering me about wearing my helmet and she'd fill our plates when we got back."

A lump came up in Sierra's throat. She missed her aunt bugging her and probably hadn't appreciated her as much as she should have. She wasn't a kid anymore and she wanted to do better with the people who were still around, which maybe even included Wyatt.

He nodded. "The diner was like my home away from home."

Her phone alarm went off. *Saved by the bell.* She hit snooze, but she wasn't ready to delve into their past. She'd promised Annie she'd get back in record time. Time to focus. She was just shaken by the encounter with that animal. Her nerves had nothing to do with how thoroughly she was drawn in by those chocolate brown eyes and that memorable scent. She needed to get back to reality.

"Yeah, I've had a few adventures myself."

The corners of Wyatt's mouth turned up. "I'd be surprised if you hadn't."

From the beginning, she purposely avoided the Fair Creek grapevine, not keeping tabs on him. Pretty easy since they had no mutual friends and didn't hang out with one another's families. Straight out of college a high-level advertising firm hired her in Cincinnati and it had been some ride, until her hearing started to become an issue.

This wasn't how she thought this would go. Sierra pulled her gaze from the man before her, looking out over the buildings on the sprawling farm. Fences, cattle, silos, all stretched as far as the eye could see on the Galloways' expansive property.

Her phone alarm went off again.

Wyatt held up his finger to wait a minute and answered his

phone. Maybe that noise hadn't been her phone?

You're seriously losing your grip, here. Or it was the hearing aids making it hard to tell where sounds originated.

She mouthed, "I'm due back at my diner," gave what she hoped was a jaunty wave, and scooted away. She kicked off at a run, pulled the van's door open and slammed it shut. Hopefully the raccoon had limited its presence to the back of her van only. But the vehicle had an appointment to get detailed and fumigated in its future, just to be safe.

She raced down the gravel lane to the main road, relaxing as her heartbeat went back to normal. Hopefully, she'd seen the last of Wyatt Galloway. She'd caught up with him and survived. Now he could float away like the dust billowing behind the van, for all she cared.

She had to admit there was something exciting about running into him the way she had, so unexpectedly. Life must be dull lately. Things had definitely been left unfinished, with loose ends, as Aunt Lucy used to say. Maybe because of the many questions that lingered about why he'd left the way he did.

But those didn't matter anymore. He didn't matter anymore. Did he?

Chapter 3

Wyatt stood at Galloway Farm wondering what had just happened. Sierra Delaney, the last person he wanted to see, had been practically driven into his arms. By a raccoon. And he'd felt like that was right where she belonged. Whoa. That fruity scent and unmistakable red hair, besides those piercing hazel-green eyes. He'd always been attracted to her and time had only made her more beautiful. They'd been close friends as kids, and he felt bad for ghosting her at prom.

Tires screeched as her van, decorated with a door magnet advertising her diner, hightailed it down the drive. His phone rang and his brother Gage's name streamed across the screen.

Something must have come up because they normally spoke at night. Calls from his brothers were his least-favorite thing. Sure, he loved them, deep down. But being thrown into business together since their father's death had downsides. Big ones. Each son had been successful in his own right and coming together in a team effort created inevitable power struggles. And Wyatt always preferred to take charge.

He waited to pick up until the last second before the call went to voice mail. "I planned to call you later," he said, projecting his voice a bit more than usual, for emphasis. "There've been a few snags and I'm set to smooth those out." He had a plan that had worked all around the country and for anyone else, that would have been enough.

Gage responded with a bellow. "Snafus are more like it or try debacle. I mean, having more than 200 people show up at a public meeting, and all but ten opposing Vortex Clean Energy when I thought it would be a slam dunk?"

"First, I own Vortex Clean Energy. You don't. Why didn't you ask me how it would go? I would have told you there would be pushback."

Wyatt strode a short way and rested his boot up on the lowest fence rung. Gage must not respect him or why would he be nosing into his business? As executor, Gage was tasked to oversee the brothers' projects, which included Caleb, and their eldest brother, Leo, as well. Dad had made special arrangements for their only sister, Kayla, and sealed them until she was well, which was clearly spelled out.

"Point taken. If I wanted to know about your business, I should have asked, and I apologize. Dad coerced me into acting as executor because he was a tightwad. He made the provisions so complicated that I wish I had turned him down."

"You're all right. Guess I overreacted. Hey, you'll never guess who I ran into today. Sierra Delaney. You wouldn't know her." At age thirty-seven as compared with Sierra's age thirty-four, they would have barely overlapped in high school.

"I feel as though I do, as much as you've talked about her."

"I don't remember it like that."

"Why do you think Dad set his will up the way he did?"

"I have ideas. But would you care to enlighten me?" Wyatt removed the phone from his ear to regroup. This kind of interaction with his family left him worked up and jumpy. He had always felt different from them, and they had spent little time together since he moved away.

Gage said, "Dad hoped we'd come back of our own accord but when he didn't see that happening, he decided not to leave it to chance. The deal lets us work with our businesses separately and put our profits toward the farm, to give us independence."

Wyatt said, "But when the attorney read us the will, you said we should do something great economically, as kind of giving back. It impressed me, aiming for such lofty goals."

Gage said, "Dad believed that. Plus, it sounded a whole lot better than saying he was reaching out from the grave to manipulate us."

Gage laughed and Wyatt did, too.

Face it, Wyatt, you jumped at the chance, to forget about Bethany's death. Their three-year marriage had been a mistake. Wyatt massaged his forehead with his fingers, closed his eyes and tried to focus on what Gage was saying.

"We actually thought seeing Sierra again might do you good."

"That was so long ago. I hadn't thought of her in years." Except this past prom season, possibly New Year's Eve, and those other times. Prom was supposed to have been their first date out of the friendship zone.

What was wrong with him? He'd regressed into high school now? Maybe coming back wasn't the best idea.

"Actually, Dad thought that leaving the way you did…seemed you didn't quite get over it. Get over her, specifically. In spite of your differences, Dad cared and wanted you to be happy."

His dad and brother as the healers of broken hearts? That didn't compute. "I'd seen that in recent years. I've concluded we didn't get along because we were so much alike."

A phone rang in the background at Gage's. "It didn't take much to get you back here, always interested in a new challenge, and you know how farm air is good for kids. Don't blame us for playing into your weaknesses."

His little boy. The mention of his thirteen-month-old, Max, had Wyatt wanting to be a better dad, a better person.

"I'd do anything for Max. You'll understand when you have kids. People claim rural living is the best. Not that it worked for me." Moving on here. "Hey, he learned his first word. 'dada.'"

"Kid must be a genius."

Gage made a lot of sense, but Wyatt's competitive nature wouldn't let him admit it. "Anyway, everything'll be fine. This doesn't have to be a permanent move. Operating in such a rural area's new for me." Delays in getting his plans approved had been just one of the frustrations.

"Don't make excuses. How different can a rural area be? There's less competition. Towns are dying out all over the state, so I expected you'd be welcomed with open arms."

Wyatt said, "Not exactly. Well, solar energy takes some special powers of persuasion. Fortunately, that's my specialty."

Gage huffed with annoyance. "You've yet to prove it in Fair Creek. Look, send me a copy of your solar research and the presentation, so I'll know exactly what's required."

"I'll send it but remember I need the demographics of Fair Creek's residents."

"Alright. And last thing, I know you were in the attorney's office with the rest of us. But it was a lot to take in. Remember we're sworn to secrecy that we're not allowed to say we're bringing some business here because of the will's provisions."

"Oh, right. He was a control freak. That's a fact. Who would I tell who would care?"

"People around here are always interested in our family and I agree with Dad. Best to keep a low profile."

"I can't wait to get back to civilization." He disconnected.

Chapter 4

After the call with Gage, Wyatt remained standing near his barn, enjoying the quiet. He didn't miss the noise of cities. He gazed out over the wide expanse of open land, all of it Galloway property. No need to let Gage know the cows in the fields and views of picture-perfect clear skies that were not blocked by buildings spoke to something inside him. Even after all the years of living away, the scene was still familiar to his core.

He thought about his faith in a positive light, not anger, for the first time in a while. He hadn't wanted to come here. But maybe there was a reason, and he just needed to trust until it presented itself. *Show me the way, Lord.*

One of the farm hands walked by, headed toward a stalled tractor way in the distance. He shoved the *Gazette* into Wyatt's hand. Wyatt frowned. "What's this.?

The guy pointed at it. "You might want to read where it's been marked up."

A photo of Sierra Delaney caught his eye and he held it closer to see it better. Even on cheap newsprint, she was the most beautiful woman he'd ever seen.

Don't go there. He could almost smell her clean, fruity scent from earlier. Things he hadn't thought about, long buried. Conversations and shared beliefs, what he'd never experienced with anyone else.

The caption underneath Sierra's photo said she was in charge of Fair Creek's economic growth council. Well, that would be a start on getting the approval he needed. It listed details for the next meeting.

He flipped through the flimsy newspaper, using the term loosely, since it had so few pages and little real news either. At the top of page two, someone had circled part of a letter to the editor. Wyatt's name jumped out at him. Wait, what was he doing in there, unless it was for his solar business? They called him a "Clothes Stallion." That was just weird. He skipped down to the bottom to see who wrote that.

He spoke out loud into the wide-open spaces. "Anonymous?" Only one person that he knew of from around here would be that clever and cutesy.

A while later, after he'd unpacked his gear and gotten things ready for Max, he watched the sky change over the course of the evening with special appreciation. Today had been full of surprises. He couldn't wait to see what came next.

Wyatt stood in his house on the farm in disbelief of how little he had gotten done the day before. But he felt more energized than he had in a long while. Max had flown in under Aunt Elizabeth's care from D.C. and the three of them had spent an entire day setting up a little boy bedroom and enjoying a visit. Recently widowed, she was vibrant and engaged in life, living in Fair Creek and willing to help family members however she could. A warmth at how blessed he was washed over him.

He and Max had both slept through the night for a change, and the toddler was all smiles when his sitter arrived. He'd awakened with a new resolve about how to deal with Sierra Delaney. Seeing her unexpectedly had thrown him off but after a day of hanging out with Max, he had a plan. She was the only one who would write a letter like that. As kids, she always scribbled in notepads and sang jingles from TV commercials. When word had gotten back to him that she'd gone into advertising, it made total sense.

Wyatt parked at the edge of town and carried the *Gazette* as he walked along, refreshing his memory of the once-familiar place. The only thing stranger than being on Fair Creek's Main Street again was how little had changed. Green-and-white-striped canvas awnings hung over each storefront, although they were faded after so long.

Not that he had thought about the place much over sixteen years, because he had been obsessed with starting a company, and growing a business that excited him in a new industry full of potential. The sky really was the limit with solar, especially getting in as early as he had. Building his empire, traveling the world, meeting with the great minds involved in the future of new energies. Those endeavors were the main reasons he hadn't come back.

Losing track of Sierra Delaney hadn't totally been a choice but more like fallout from how career-driven he'd been. A twitch of regret clung to him at the thought of her name.

Attending Dad's services at the funeral home on Fair Creek's edge six months ago hadn't seemed real. He swallowed the lump in his throat. When Mom had been alive, she'd insisted on occasional trips out to see Wyatt and brought his dad. That's when he'd realized they were too alike to get along very well. They'd built some bridges though, and he had hoped for more down the road.

His gaze connected with the church steeple rising above the town, where he'd attended starting as a young child. That was before he'd left.

Lately he'd been thinking how his life would have been different if he'd stayed. Or if he'd come back for holidays even. *Lord, I'm here now. What would you have me do?*

"Hey, Wyatt. What do you know?"

He turned toward the sound just in time. A man in a golf cart sped down the middle of the street.

"Not much, Ted!"

Ted slowed his speed and Wyatt didn't want to get into a long chat, which happened so often in small towns, from what he'd heard. You didn't have to worry about that type of thing when you lived in Washington, D.C. He waved as though he didn't intend to talk, and Ted pulled the cart into a parallel parking spot and strode into Delaney's.

Wyatt halted at the town's only stoplight, feeling the day's heat begin to come up through his cowboy boots. Normal 10 a.m. stuff for another scorching-hot July day. Shifting the *Gazette* into his other hand, Wyatt crossed the street, shoved open the door of the convenience store and went in.

He couldn't believe he was abandoning the strategy he'd adopted when he'd started trips back to the family farm a few weeks ago. Avoiding Sierra Delaney hadn't worked, thanks to a ringtail. Now he intended to confront her. Signed or not, she'd written that letter about him to the editor.

He grabbed a pack of his favorite gum, as a pick-me-up. His motto had always been to never let anybody see him sweat. The philosophy applied double when it came to Sierra.

The cashier rang up his purchase and he was about to pay when he spotted a miniature black stallion in the sea of useless plastic items for sale. He snatched up the animal and paid for it too. If Sierra had made fun of him, and he was 99.9% sure she had, based on their history together, he wanted her to be as uncomfortable as he was.

Back on the sidewalk, long strides took him a few feet past the barbershop, A Cut Above, where he stopped to examine the familiar Delaney's sign. Being here was like stepping back in time.

When he was a boy, he and his father would get haircuts and then they'd grab a bite to eat at the diner. An image of holding his dad's hand to cross the street, when he was a young boy, flitted through Wyatt's mind along with a long-forgotten feeling of warmth and security. It was the teen years when things had gotten rough between them.

The letter in the paper about how he dressed was no big deal and would be more of an irritation to most people. But it had touched a nerve. When he'd left town, he'd been strapped for money and couldn't afford these clothes or anything close. He ran his finger underneath the starched collar, made of premium cotton fabric that was sticking to his neck in the humid weather. The education to get him here had been far from easy.

In two long strides, he pulled open the door, and stepped into the diner on a worn rug. From his corner of the room, he noted that several of the vinyl seats had slight tears. He prided himself on thinking of everything from a perspective of assets, liabilities, and profits. These issues not only marred the appearance of the business, but someone could fall and might file a lawsuit. Cracked plastic could harbor germs. Boy, living in the city for fifteen years had played with his mind, if he couldn't appreciate an old-fashioned diner.

The aroma of meat cooking on the grill, fried onion rings, and coffee enveloped him, as well as the laughter and nostalgic conversations that swirled around. Nobody's eyes were fixated on phone screens. People were gathered in around their coffee cups chatting instead of running in to grab drinks and go. The good times he had spent there flooded back, of getting a milkshake after school and hanging out. The warm, welcoming atmosphere hadn't changed. He supposed the Delaney family should be given credit for that.

He would have kept his vow never to see her again if Dad's will hadn't basically forced them all to come back. Seeing her had opened a window that had remained shut until now. He came here due to legal papers. And to give Max a chance to taste small-town life. There was no other reason, in spite of what Gage thought about him never getting over Sierra.

She worked the counter where she couldn't see him. Just a glimpse of her in her family diner made him wish for a slower pace for himself and Max. Replacing the rat race of city life full of upscale restaurants and traffic, with a substitution of drives through the country, tending horses, and having a town parade, answered some need within him. It stretched his imagination to think Sierra would be any part of that. Although they had only been friends when he left, there had been a conversation about becoming more. Sixteen years ago, and a lot of living in between made that unlikely. They might not be in the same stage in life.

A boy needed more than a community though. He needed a mother. But that was a tall order and coming here felt like a new start, and a good one. He wouldn't risk making another mistake in the relationship department, which essentially meant avoiding dating altogether. He didn't trust himself, since he had a pattern of misinterpreting the motivations of the women he'd been involved with and that included Bethany, whom he'd walked down the aisle with.

"How does next month at Delaney's sound?" asked a woman a couple of decades older than his thirty-five years. She pulled out a small paper calendar as she sat at a table with three others, chatting over salads. An image of Mom planning a future meeting of one of her ladies' clubs, formed in his mind. Something in him stirred, cherishing those days. Simply being around the people in this room made him feel better somehow.

"Let's go, before they start charging us rent." Ted Mitchell got up to leave with several guys he'd sipped coffee with. There was something genuine about their interactions, such as a quick pat on the arm in parting, even in how they tidied up their table and placed their cups on top of the trash container. Maybe drinking from glazed ceramic mugs like Ted and his friends used wouldn't impact the taste of his chosen beverage but wrapping his hand around something solid instead of a to-go cup had to be more satisfying. When was the last time he'd sat in a restaurant without the pressing need to be somewhere else in the back of his mind? At home in D.C., he'd practically worn a walking path from his car door to inside his favorite specialty coffee shop and the spot designated for picking up online orders.

When Sierra smiled at a customer, her inner spirit drew him. What would it be like to have someone beside him when he didn't know what to do for Max? Or when Max needed more nurturing than he could give. Or just for himself. Was "Doting Dad" going to be his only role? But she had been difficult to read at the farm over that coon, when he'd caught a glint of happiness to see him at some point, and uncertainty at other times.

Behind the counter, she waited on a customer, with a smile on her face. Something twisted in his chest. What if he could find what he'd wanted all along, with her?

Don't be ridiculous. The fresh, smog-free air must be getting to him.

Chapter 5

Sierra stood at the Delaney's counter with a vice grip on her pen, not sure why she was on edge. A mother and her young son were deciding on their order when she noticed a sticky note on the register. The word "passport" written on it reminded her of a marketing idea she'd heard of when she worked at the advertising agency.

The mother and son ordered and she took care of them.

Next, Natalie Bogue, director of Fair Creek Community's tiny church choir, shifted over in line. "Hey, Sierra, I'll have a tin roof sundae."

"Great choice! I remember when Mom convinced Aunt Lucy that Spanish nuts weren't too expensive to buy because she thought tin roofs would be popular. She was right."

"What a neat story. This whole place is a testament to your

family. They would be so proud of you for keeping it going."

Comments like hers were part of the reason she kept trying. She made quick work of putting together a dish of soft serve with hot fudge and Spanish peanuts.

She had customers this afternoon, an improvement. Looking out the picture window, she could almost see steam rising off the pavement, it was so hot. Most had come in for ice cream, so their food tickets weren't large. But she'd take what she could get. A picture of Aunt Lucy on the wall, from this angle, appeared as though she were looking right at Sierra.

It didn't seem real that the diner was hers alone. So were the debts, unfortunately. All the good memories would need to pull her through. The fact that Aunt Lucy had also been the woman who raised her after her mother passed made the ache in her heart deeper. Dad sending her to be with Aunt Lucy was an act of love and sacrifice.

I'm doing the best I can, Auntie. She had always been there for Sierra and she wouldn't let her dream die.

"Look alive there, ladies. What's the scoop? Get it? You sell ice cream?" Shirley Leap, her friend and classmate who owned Beadangled, stood at the counter.

Sierra stopped herself from rolling her eyes about the corny joke. "Great to see you. You just missed our regulars. They're the ones who've got all the news. Get it, the 'scoop?'"

Naturally curly blonde hair cascaded to Shirley's shoulders and radiated like a halo around her head. "Point made. No one's as witty as they think, huh?"

Shirley picked up a *Gazette* newspaper on the counter from the stack left there for customers. "Did you see that funny Letter to the Editor this week?"

Sierra stopped ringing up seven orders Shirley had placed for the ladies at her weekly beading class. The two of them had been close since meeting in fourth grade when Sierra asked if her hair was real.

Just let it go. Sierra resumed working the register. "Which one? The gerbil who ran away whose owner's offering a reward?"

"Are you kidding? Haven't you read it? The Clothes Stallion one."

"I've had a busy week."

Shirley put the paper back on the stack. "Last night's beading class had a heyday with it. They're thinking about creating a beaded sign of a Clothes Stallion. I don't know what's wrong with Anonymous. I'd have no qualms about getting to know a Clothes Horse. At this point, I'd settle for a Clothes Pony."

"That's no surprise, coming from a 35-year-old woman who skates in the street and named her daughter after a children's book character from the 60s."

"Speaking of which, Amelia's art class is creating animatronic characters. They can choose from a clothes horse or anything with a cat."

Amelia was her twelve-year-old daughter with her late husband Will, who had been her college sweetheart and died of cancer.

Sierra corralled her thoughts and paused for a moment. Was

her teasing a code method of saying she knew Sierra had written the letter? While deciding whether to confess, she looked up and couldn't miss the trademark dark hair and the once-familiar profile of Wyatt Galloway. He stood at the blackboard menu. Her heartbeat quickened. Tall, dark, and handsome. He'd been six-foot two when she knew him, but Delaney's low ceiling made him seem even taller, or maybe he'd had a growth spurt after he left. He hadn't set foot in her place in sixteen years, so he must have a reason. She inhaled a breath and shooed Shirley out the door.

Chapter 6

Sierra stood at the counter at Delaney's and vowed not to have a meltdown now that Wyatt was heading her way. Trying to look casual, she reached up and fluffed the tendrils from her ponytail to make sure both hearing aids were covered. It was a new habit, but she couldn't stop. Too soon, Wyatt stood in front of her. His intense brown eyes locked with hers. His expression was unreadable.

She couldn't take her eyes off of his gorgeous face underneath his cowboy hat, still dressed in a designer business suit. Her heart thumped as if it might come out of her chest. Had he seen the newspaper? Would he believe it was all a mistake?

"Sierra." He hesitated a couple of seconds. She gulped and wondered if suspense could kill a person. "I'll take a Lucy Burger, fries and a pop." His attitude was all business. She worried about what kind of business.

She could deal with anything, if only her mouth weren't so dry.

"Would you like extras added to the burger?"

"No. Just what comes with." His voice had definitely deepened since she'd known him long ago. She didn't need hearing aids to appreciate that. A whiff of his woodsy scent took her way, way back.

She glanced at the man waiting in line next to Wyatt.

What did it matter if he overheard her? "I always thought I might deck you if I ever saw you again." Under the brim of his cowboy hat, his eyes grew wide as she continued. "But I own this place and have responsibilities now. And you did save me from that beast."

The corners of his mouth twitched up. "I'll be sure to thank him when I see him around."

She shuddered. "Better you than me."

Putting down her pen, she rang up his order and he paid. Their fingers brushed as she handed over his change. A spark of warmth travelled up her arm.

She pulled away and slammed the cash drawer harder than she'd meant to. Wyatt turned, started to step away. Something she couldn't identify, a longing maybe, came over her.

Then he stopped. "When things slow down, come back to my table. I'd like to talk to you."

She nodded, hoping her eyes didn't give her away. Give away what, she wasn't sure. That she was curious about him but wary of him too?

A child in a corner spilled a drink and she wiped it up. Once the dining room was cleared, she strolled to the back where he sat, his cowboy hat on the table, designer suit jacket draped over a chair.

She could do business as well as he could. "How's your meal? Can we get you anything else?"

"What, you're a split personality now?"

She stifled a smile. "Me, myself, and I."

Wyatt rubbed his hands together a couple of times, like he used to in new situations. At least she wasn't the only one out of her element here. Too bad they didn't have a road map for meeting again after a huge gap in a friendship that ended badly. Never at a loss for words that she could remember, he seemed to be having trouble this time.

"I'll get right to the point." He paused, though.

Her gaze went to a little plastic horse sitting on the table, its mane flowing out behind as though blowing in the wind.

"My cousin's daughter has a horse in her farm set. You have a play date?"

He shook his head. A stray lock of hair fell onto his forehead. She wanted to brush it off his forehead, to touch him.

What was wrong with her?

"It's a stallion," he said. "My personal mascot. Picked it up at the convenience store on my way over."

She chewed on her lip and felt her cheeks flush as she tried to form words.

When they had been best friends in high school, they had never fought. He tossed the toy back and forth and didn't hide his irritation.

"What kind of newspaper runs an unsigned rant about somebody who's come to town after years away?"

She shrugged. "Is this the bonus round so I need to answer in the form of a question? What is…a free weekly, desperate for copy?"

He plunked the toy down on the table.

"Horses seem to be a popular topic, if the *Gazette* is to be believed…" Her voice cracked halfway through, and she stopped.

He picked up the toy as though he didn't notice she might keel over from lack of oxygen and ran his large hand over the horse's back. Her stomach flip-flopped.

She'd always admired his long, lean fingers. "I didn't think name calling would be your style," he said.

"How would *you* know?" How dare he assume he still knew her. Well, he didn't. Nope. Not anymore.

He formed his hamburger wrapper into a ball, tucked it into the paper bag. "Who else would be clever enough to come up with the term Clothes Stallion but someone in advertising? You always played with words and had a unique sense of humor."

What? How would he know about her former career, before the diner? She'd worked a successful advertising job in Cincinnati. "Anyone can see you're dressed way too classy for this rural town, Wyatt."

He fiddled with the toy while he talked. "For a friendly town,

Fair Creek sure has some unfriendly ways about it. Those yard signs people posted with an 'X' over 'Solar Farm' aren't exactly welcoming."

She shifted her weight from one foot to the other.

Wyatt studied her, and she couldn't help but be mesmerized by those deep-brown eyes, like home-brewed coffee, and his unique style. He had earned the Clothes Stallion nickname with that tailored dark suit and perfectly fitted dress shirt on his frame, in addition to the graceful way he carried himself. How could she have forgotten the gold flecks in his eyes? Butterflies launched into a full-out dance in her stomach.

His jaw remained set in a rigid line. When he spoke, his grumpy tone broke the spell. "Coming up with nicknames was your favorite thing. I instinctively knew it was you."

What could she say when nothing seemed adequate?

He had enough to say for both of them. "*You* might think it's cute. But when I'm needing the community to back my plan, in the process of a marketing campaign…"

Her ad instincts kicked in. "The paper has such a small circulation that something like this won't have any impact. I'm surprised you read it."

"Someone brought it to my attention. You've opted out of corporate life but surely the information age hasn't passed you by. All it takes is one person hitting 'like' on the internet to create more circulation than the newspaper has ever had. It's all over social media."

"Really? Congratulations. I know I've always wanted to go

viral. Doesn't everybody?" Every ad pro she'd ever known did. She picked up her phone and did a search. "You're right. There's a publication with a massive online following that's posted it."

"This is supposed to make me feel better? Look, I know you had something to do with this. Even if it was indirectly, you know what they say, 'It's the thought that counts.'"

"I'm sorry this town is giving you a hard time, Wyatt." She had intentionally phrased it so she didn't admit guilt. "They also say, if the shoe fits." She looked down to his fine-leather cowboy boots. *Everything looks good on you.*

"Are those Italian?"

A smile flitted across his face as he nodded. "Italy's one of my favorite countries. I broke down and bought a villa to match."

They'd talked about riding gondolas in Venice as kids. They'd come from a tiny town, but were big dreamers.

He had a quizzical expression she couldn't interpret. Maybe he remembered, too.

Back in the day, she would have tried to figure out what that look meant. But she kept quiet as he tucked the toy into his pocket.

When he spoke again, his grumpy tone had returned. "Look, the damage is done. I've thought of a way for you to make it up to me, though."

Chapter 7

Sierra looked across the table at Wyatt, not believing what he'd just said. "But I don't owe you anything."

No truer words had ever been spoken. She owed the man nothing and definitely wouldn't be trying to make amends. They glared at one another for what seemed like hours but it had to be less than a minute. He was delusional. She would not apologize, which would have to start with admitting she did something, which she had no intention of doing. He'd never said he was sorry for cutting out of town without saying goodbye to her. And leaving her letters and calls unanswered had been even worse.

"By belittling me in the paper, I'm going to have less influence, in some people's eyes. There are people who really do believe everything they read." He spread the *Gazette* out on the table, with her photo and the caption about her role in the council squarely in front of her. "We're rebranding to Galloway Sons Farm and working on projects, pulling together now that Dad's gone. Solar panels are my area of expertise and I've started the public discussion to bring them here. You're in charge of the economic growth council and I could use your endorsement."

"And if I don't support you?"

"I'll let the stallion out of the bag and tell everyone you undermined my business by writing that absurd letter, the opposite of what you claim to do on the council."

"It's been said, 'There's no such thing as bad publicity.'"

She didn't love the idea of him letting people know and chose to think no one would see his leaking of her letter either, let alone devote any of their attention to it. But sometimes Fair Creek seemed to specialize in pettiness. The townspeople were never more unified than when they were opposing something. Unfortunately for him, this year they were rejecting solar panels.

But he didn't need to know all that. "No one will care. You've said yourself that everyone's against your solar business." It wasn't her fault people around here were skeptical about solar panels. "I won't promote something I don't believe in myself."

"The Fair Creek economy could really benefit. I'm asking you to help them see me in a better light, so they'll listen to my message and review the advantages. Places all over the country, towns with farms just like Fair Creek, are embracing solar."

His eyes lit up when he talked about his business. He had always come alive when they had shared their goals. A thread of attraction ratcheted up in her, at seeing him so animated. They had worked closely together before, getting themselves voted onto the student senate and raising funds for the out-of-state marching band trip. She'd forgotten all about that.

"Let me show you. I'll give my personal presentation to you, you alone, to start off."

Bringing in new businesses to Fair Creek had been the foundation of the council. It had been her idea, but it was more of a concept than an actual thing at this point. "Put a lid on any of your expectations. The council's just getting going—"

"Don't be modest, Sierra. You're the closest thing Fair Creek's got to a mayor." Sierra nearly jumped. Annie had stopped beside their table with a handful of napkins. After opening the dispenser, Annie found it already full, then stood there and beamed a smile at Wyatt.

Sierra said, "I thought you were leaving early."

Annie flipped her long blonde hair over her shoulder, a habit she seemed to have developed lately. Maybe she'd gotten it by osmosis from her. Or else they were both stressing out about various situations. "Oh, well, things changed. Caleb didn't need me with the twins after all and he was going to see a lawyer. Let's say I'm at loose ends. All my cleaning's done, for once. All I'm going to do anyway."

Sierra swallowed, trying to tamp down her own emotions as she directed her attention to Wyatt. Drew and Ella were her babies, too, to some extent. Ever since Caleb became the twins' guardian because Kayla was addicted to drugs, the whole town had fallen in love with them. She didn't have any answers to offer about the attorney but knew the one who did. "All we can do is pray about the babies. For God's will in their lives."

Annie's eyes shimmered with tears. She moved on to the next table's napkin dispenser.

Wyatt's eyes were more intensely brown somehow, in a way she didn't recognize.

He nodded. She wished she could help. What if they all became family, since her cousin might potentially be marrying his brother? They needed to get along. "Honestly, Fair Creek wants to become pro-business, but we're not quite there yet. I saw on the internet your company is thriving in lots of other places already."

She looked over at the door. Please, where were her customers, to make her money and to cut short this conversation? Unfortunately, for all that she tried, afternoons were still her slow time.

He rubbed his hands together. "It's complicated. Anyway, I didn't expect this to be easy. We've had to fight and educate the public in every place we've gone. But I'm hearing negative rumblings more than I'd like."

The bell on the door jangled and she sagged with relief. Even after the way he'd left, and treated her afterward, she was going to have trouble saying no to Wyatt Galloway. His family had a lot of clout. They were all regulars at her business when they came into town. She catered for them. She would need to tread carefully.

A young woman in a T-shirt with a community college's logo from the next town over almost waddled in, she was so loaded down carrying a little boy and a car seat, with a diaper bag over one shoulder. Sierra moved toward the counter to wait on them. But the woman passed her by and spoke to Wyatt.

"I've got to get some studying done. Summer school's intense. Who ever heard of a thirteen-month-old that gave up on naps?"

Sierra couldn't look away from the child's wispy hair the color of Wyatt's and those same brown eyes. There was no doubt whose he was. And her heart lurched at the idea of a mini-Wyatt, because even though it had nothing to do with her, her hidden ache, the one where she wanted a baby, floated to the surface.

"Hi, Big Guy," Wyatt said.

The child's whole face lit up when he smiled and reached out and Mr. Clothes Stallion took him without a thought for his pressed white shirt. *When would he take the hint and dress like a cowboy?*

He leaned in to kiss the little head, and patted his son's arm, then moved in for the target and tickled his tummy.

Sierra's heart swelled at seeing father and son together. Her stomach tightened. She should have known Wyatt would be married, but why hadn't Annie told her? Maybe because Sierra shut down any conversation about the Galloways, before it had begun, unless it was related to her business.

Why do you care anyway?

Her cousin was probably too busy with Caleb and the babies to think about much else. Sierra had made a point of not talking about Caleb with Annie much at all.

She definitely hadn't told Annie how Wyatt's leaving had

devastated her. They were close. Annie knew all about her hearing aids, the only person she'd really let in. Yet Sierra had stopped short of telling her how self-conscious they made her.

"Sierra, this is Max. And this is Kylie. I posted an ad for college students at Haven University to take shifts babysitting. There are background checks." Wyatt turned to the woman "I'm nearly finished here."

Good. I'm ready to be done here.

Kylie hung her head. "I'm really sorry about this."

"It's fine." Wyatt's smile didn't reach his eyes. "I understand that you need to go. Thank you for taking care of Max today. Why don't you order your dinner here? I'll pay for it on my way out. We'll see you tomorrow, won't we?" He waved at her and Max imitated him.

Kyle paused. "Oh, and on the way over, the radio announcer read parts of the newspaper. Thought you might want to know that somebody called you a Clothes Stallion. Guess they needed something to fill their time on-air?" She grinned, and when he didn't react, she shrugged.

"Thanks for letting me know." Wyatt turned to Sierra.

She avoided eye contact, making herself busy arranging the condiments on the table while Annie went to take care of Kylie's order. Sierra didn't want it to look like she was trying to get away from Wyatt.

Wyatt dragged his gaze from Max. Or could he be reluctant to look at her, too? What was she going to do about his request for help? He was going to ask again. She just knew it.

"Do you have baby ice cream cups?" *That* was what he wanted to know? He must be in full dad mode now.

"Of course, we do. How about homemade vanilla soft serve made with all natural ingredients?"

Getting that letter out in the open had taken the edge off her mood but it was short lived. Now she'd moved onward to dreading the potential of being associated with his solar business.

Relief for the change of topic flooded through her. That baby needed ice cream, and he was her littlest customer. Since she was eight and hanging around with her aunt at the diner, she had been comfortable with taking care of customers. It wasn't Max's fault she had issues with his dad.

Without warning, the little guy lunged over the table, reaching for Sierra. She automatically stretched both arms out to receive him.

Her voice gentle, she addressed the baby directly. "You want to come with me. Can't wait for me to bring you the ice cream?"

Max's big brown eyes studied her. With Max leaning in Sierra's direction, Wyatt handed him to her. She leaned in close to his sweet head and inhaled the scent of mild soap and that unnamed, yet unmistakable all-baby aroma she knew from years of babysitting. Wyatt offered his hands to Max, trying to coax him back.

"Let Sierra make your ice cream in peace."

Max's eyes twinkled as he looked at Wyatt but he wasn't having it. Wyatt's cell phone rang. He checked the number.

"I better take this." He spoke firmly. "Come here, Max."

Max brushed his face on Sierra's sleeve. She waved Wyatt off and smiled at the baby. Before the phone went to voice mail, she shot a question toward Wyatt. "So what's Daddy's favorite flavor?"

"Something butterscotch." Wyatt answered the phone and Sierra moved toward the counter.

Her cousin had just finished cleaning up after serving Kylie. "I'm out of here," Annie said.

"Oh, just when the real work starts. I see how it is."

Annie grinned. "My most important job is done, promoting you as town mayor, I mean, council president." She headed toward the employee exit, giving no time for Sierra to mount a protest.

Standing at the ice cream machine, Max's weight against her was more comfortable than she expected. She swayed where she stood and his eyes fluttered a little. A swirl filled the small cup and then she made a sundae sized for Wyatt. By the time she had made his and ladled on a scoop of the warm butterscotch, her junior helper's head was on her shoulder, eyes closed, lips parted.

Babies.

She'd always loved being around them. His sweet scent combined with the sugary butterscotch filled her senses.

Max's lashes were long against his cheeks. What would it be like if he were hers?

That would never be. But a girl could dream for a minute, couldn't she? She put both bowls of ice cream on a tray and went back into the dining room.

Chapter 8

"I really appreciate your thinking of me," Wyatt said, trying to wind down the call with Aunt Elizabeth. Out of the corner of his eye, he watched Sierra's progress with the ice cream. This didn't seem real, to be at Delaney's again after all this time. Let alone that Max was in Sierra's arms and looked like he belonged there. Dad's will had directed him to come back to Fair Creek so he had. Being drawn to the place was unexpected and a little unsettling.

Aunt Elizabeth continued to ramble. She'd been widowed about a year and a half ago. After all his time away, she'd welcomed him back and he always found it difficult to get her off of the phone. "Like I said, we had some rides in the Fourth of July parade cancel last-minute. Will you be a substitute and ride one of your horses, to let everyone know you're back?" she said. "But, um, you're probably aware there's talk about your solar project in town, so some of them already know."

"Word has a way of getting around," he said.

"But you'll look so handsome on that horse!" Sierra came closer with a sleeping Max as she made her way toward him carrying the ice cream on a tray.

"I'm happy to help. Email me the details and I'll be there in full cowboy gear." Maybe he should dress a little more like he belonged here. "Aunt Elizabeth, I've really got to go now."

As Sierra placed the tray on the table, Max's eyes flew open. She transferred him to Wyatt and hauled a highchair over for the baby. Wyatt put Max in his chair and Sierra stayed nearby until he had the strap secured. The fruity scent of her hair wafted to him, making him wish things had been different.

He sat down. She sat down across from him and he did a double-take. He wanted her there—if she wanted to be–and yet he didn't. It was like a flashback to when they'd been in Delaney's years ago. The slowness of the town, as compared with D.C., made it seem unimportant to figure everything out right away.

"Don't you want ice cream?

She shook her head. "Working here has curbed my interest quite a bit. I hope you don't mind my joining you. He's beautiful," she said, her cheeks flushed with the admission.

"You won't get any argument from me, about sitting here or your thoughts on Max."

She spooned ice cream to Max and Wyatt dug into his. He'd missed having a woman fawn over Max. He'd delivered the message about what he expected from her and needed to stay on safe topics now.

"Looks like I'm going to be riding in the parade."

Her smile as she looked at Max lit up her face. He'd forgotten her dimples.

"That'll be fun. Delaney's traditionally entered a float, but not this year."

She didn't look happy about it. For some reason, he wished he could bring back her smile.

He recognized the impulse to save someone, or whatever it was, from when he'd met Bethany, Max's mother. She'd been intense and had mood swings that he tried to help her with. And look how badly that had turned out.

He hated to break their spell of getting along but business was never far from his mind.

"If you help me turn things around with my company image, I'll get on board with building up the economic council."

She paused to give Max another bite.

"That's generous of you. Given the circumstances, I'm not sure if that's a good idea." She shrugged and he got the impression she didn't want to define the circumstances. She could mean their past, or the fact his business was unpopular.

"I won't be helping without thinking it over first," she said. "Frankly, I'm amazed at how you do it all, with Max, too? That's a lot for two working parents. At least, I assumed your wife works."

The simple answer he always gave formed in his mind. Looking into those hazel eyes stopped him. He considered giving her the full story and not just the facts, then decided against it. Their past made him feel close to her sooner than he normally would.

"His mom died soon after having him."

Her face fell and her eyes opened wide. People were usually shocked but she seemed deeply bothered. She opened her mouth and covered it with her hand.

After composing herself, she spoke. "I'm sorry for your loss and feel terrible for Max. My mom died when I was fifteen and it changed my life. You were there for the early part of my grieving process."

He wondered what she would say if she knew the truth, that he and Max's mother didn't have a happy marriage. Without warning, Max's hand darted out and swiped at the wispy hair around Sierra's face. A look came into her eyes. He couldn't tell if it was fear or something else. Everything in him wanted to ask but he'd given up that right the night he left. She gently moved the little hand away, then scooted over and fluffed her hair.

She'd never been prissy and he didn't know what to make of it.

"We manage, sometimes just barely, though," he said. Might as well be honest. He was no saint of a dad but he tried. "Once he's in a routine, he'll sleep. The community college students I have caring for him here all take different shifts. When we were in D.C., we had a nanny. And I haven't found a nanny with the qualifications I'm looking for who wants to live in Fair Creek, Indiana. I've enjoyed spending more time with him than I have before, since the pace is slower here."

She nodded.

They looked at Max, who appeared to enjoy having their attention. He opened his rosebud mouth. He fought to keep his sparkling eyes open as he took the last little bite of ice cream.

"Look, I've got to get him home. This has been nice. Not to bring up a strained subject, but are you going to make things right and put me in a better light for my solar business? You'll be helping the town at the same time."

She stood and stepped back, as if she intentionally wanted to put distance between them. "I won't make any promises."

He put the diaper bag on his shoulder, made quick work of getting Max in his car seat. "You'd take a chance on everyone knowing you wrote that awful letter?"

"I won't be pressured into it. You've changed, Wyatt."

"Of course, I have. Life has its way of shaping us as we work our way through what it throws at us. God doesn't promise it'll be easy, only that he'll be with us. In some things, I'm just glad I made it out the other side."

He'd said his piece, for better or worse.

"Everyone's life has some sad chapters, Wyatt. The point is to use what you've been through to help somebody else."

"That's something to aim for. I'm going to have to work my way out of my current situation first."

"I think you're overstating the impact the letter has. Maybe I'll leak it to people that I did it as a joke."

Would she really do that? Bringing it up again would only

prolong its life.

"That's one option. But I was talking about the bigger picture, about whether Max and I will make our home here. Goodbye, Sierra." He stalked off.

His pulse was up as he moved away from her. He would focus on the personal. Sierra had been great with Max. Wyatt simply had to find a way for his son to spend more time with nurturing women. The way the two of them had naturally responded to one another was something all his money couldn't buy in a nanny. But maybe he could come close.

She'd had a point that they should think twice about working together under the circumstances. When they sparred on separate sides, he felt even more drawn to her.

Chapter 9

Wyatt pulled away from Delaney's in the classic sedan of Dad's he'd been driving when he came to Fair Creek. Max hadn't stirred since he'd tucked him into his car seat, and he put the radio on low as a farm news station spewed corn and soybean prices. After switching to a music station, a love ballad tugged at his heartstrings. He reached out to the knob to change again when he stopped. The lyrics he and Sierra used to listen to and sang along with floated into the car.

Great. He really had her on the brain now. Going to Delaney's to meet her, where they had gone every day after school, wasn't his best idea.

Face it, wherever you met up with her, she'd have the same effect on you. She was beautiful as ever, more so now that she was an adult woman. He'd never seen anyone with eyes the shade of

Sierra's.

He tapped hard on the brakes, because daydreaming meant he'd nearly missed seeing a stop sign, then glanced to be sure he hadn't disturbed Max. His son continued to sleep, unaware of how Wyatt needed to get a grip. But thinking about her voice and when their hands had accidentally touched lingered, a reaction that reminded him of crushes he had in school. Only they had just been good friends, and high school was far in his rearview mirror.

Straighten up. You've got Dad's will to contend with and Max needs to get settled in. Would she help him open up Fair Creek's citizens' minds to what he had to say?

How could he be thinking that? Even if he'd wanted to smooth things out with her, he didn't trust himself to be in another relationship, not after he'd been so wrong about Bethany. Before her, there was another ill-fated relationship. He didn't think he could ever let someone in again.

His cell rang. He reacted quickly as Caleb's name flashed across, not wanting to disturb Max. "Hello?"

"Where are you? Not at home, I noticed."

He could tell in his tone that Caleb wasn't his usual chipper self.

"You checking up on me now?"

Hopefully, it hadn't come out as grouchy as he suspected it had. He didn't know how to deal with relationships, and not just with women. The fall-out of leaving the way he had all those years ago, meant he was playing catch up with his brothers.

"Wanted to be sure I didn't miss the call to come post bail or something."

Ouch.

"Yeah, well I've kept clean for around twenty years but you do you." Now he was the one irritated and didn't care that it showed. Some things just weren't funny.

It was just like his brother to bring up something he wanted to forget but also possibly needed to discuss with Sierra, depending how things progressed. The night he'd left her at prom, he and Dad's butting heads turned into a physical fight. An off-duty policeman had spotted the brief skirmish, called it in and they had cooperated instantly.

"Hey, I was out of line, sorry. I'm looking for you, thinking maybe you'd want to come by. We could have a laundry session." Caleb laughed. "Never seen so many little clothes in my life. Twins, love them to pieces. They're work."

"Sure. Max is asleep. You have a place I can let him sleep while we visit?"

"I'm all set up for him. Annie insisted."

"Okay, sounds good. Be there in ten."

He wished Caleb had not brought up a tortured memory that now reeled through his mind. The two cops had gotten after John Galloway to press charges, said Wyatt needed to be taught a lesson, but Dad had refused. Maybe Wyatt should have been grateful. But the words exchanged and what had gone down had him going back home sulking, packing a few things, and by the time the family was up in the morning, he'd been long gone. He'd been too caught up in his anger and the moment to consider Sierra.

Wyatt pulled up to Caleb's, gathered Max and his baby gear, then went into the main house Caleb had claimed after their father died. He couldn't blame Caleb, since he would have done the same thing, and the place Wyatt ended up with was plenty big enough for him and Max. At dusk, the two structures were close enough that it was easy to tell if anyone was home, from either brother's place. Before Wyatt got to the door, Caleb opened it and held it for him so he could get in without jostling Max.

"You make a great door man. I appreciate it."

Caleb laughed, which was exactly what Wyatt aimed for. "Glad I'm good for something."

Maybe there was hope for him being more than a "solar genius" as that media outlet had named him. It was time for some personal-relationship practice.

None of the Galloways were negative, except he knew he could get out of sorts sometimes, like now. Sierra hadn't agreed to his plan like he wanted her to, so a visit with Caleb would be a great distraction. Wyatt studied Caleb, possibly the most upbeat of the brothers. He looked a bit mussed, hair standing up, circles under his eyes. "You're probably good for a couple of things. Give me a sec. Let me think…"

Max snoozed, so he parked him in his car seat in the corner of the room and tucked a light blanket around him.

Caleb brought a mug of steaming coffee. "Want some?"

He held up his hand in a stop motion. "Too late for me. If

the big guy sleeps, I don't want to be caffeinated to where I can't enjoy catching some Z's."

Caleb took a deep sip. "With two, I don't have a chance." He glanced at the baby monitor, which was propped on the table in a pile of onesies, rompers, and T-shirts. Wyatt had a moment of pride that he knew the terminology of baby clothes.

Caleb didn't look very relaxed, based on pacing around the room and looking out the window at the moon. "Ella and Drew went down early so who knows what that means for later? Anyway, thanks for coming."

Wyatt shrugged. "Couldn't come up with an excuse not to since I was already headed to your neighborhood. Honestly, if I were in your shoes, I would hire a nanny. Importing one from wherever you can source them and paying outrageously might save your sanity."

Caleb checked that Max was asleep before chuckling more softly than Wyatt thought he normally did. "That might be a permanent solution to a temporary situation. Besides, if I really get worn down, Annie comes over and spots them for me so I can get some sleep."

"There's so much loaded into what you just said. Your kids maybe not permanently living with you. Annie in your life. And I can count on Max needing something soon, probably a fresh diaper. I'd like to be at home when I do that. If there's anything on your mind other than needing a laundry buddy, better dive in."

Caleb took the next few minutes to outline what his attorney had told him about the twins. Kayla had her ups and downs so nothing had improved a great deal. Caleb was grappling with whether to approach her to let him start the process to adopt her children.

He folded small clothes and put them into piles as he talked. "Caring for them is the most difficult situation I've ever been in. Not because of them. They're a joy. The responsibility overwhelms me at times. If I were their biological father, it would be different. It's like I'm in the middle and have been given the duty of deciding who should parent them. Kayla knows she is messing up and she does love them and want what's best for them. She might even let me adopt them, which would ease my mind from wondering about what my role will be in their future. She's only twenty-five years old. It's a rough decision to make and I worry she'll stop trying if she doesn't have the possibility of being with them as her goal." He gulped coffee from his mug.

Wyatt rubbed his hands together, ill-equipped to know how to respond. Caleb looked like he could burst into tears and Wyatt couldn't guarantee he wouldn't join him. Losing Max would devastate him and the twins were like Caleb's own children.

Wyatt inhaled and let his breath out slowly. "You aren't alone. I know what it's like in the middle of the night, wrestling with struggles. We're here for you. I wasn't there in the past but I am now. Whatever happens, you'll get through it. I've watched you become a terrific dad and have full confidence you'll do whatever is necessary and in their best interest, whatever sacrifices it might entail for you."

"That makes me feel better. I play in my mind all the scenarios, the 'what ifs' that drive me crazy."

"Having Max has brought me back to God and prayer comforts me when questions arise. I will say this. Kayla's our baby sister and I hate to think what I knew when I was twenty-five. Her addiction, how she stole from Dad. Those are things I mull over. I don't know what could have been done differently but if you're right and she'll give up, I think you have your answer. As difficult as uncertainty is for you, don't move forward with an adoption, if you could even convince her to give up rights. If she's at a low point, she might give them up only because she is down on herself."

He'd had some low times and knew what it was like to think that they would never end.

Max let out a chirp. Caleb gave Wyatt a wide-eyed look. Wyatt thought his step seemed a bit lighter when he walked over and set his empty cup in the sink. "That all makes sense. I'll take the time the lawyer recommended and make my decision."

Max made another sound and Wyatt stood. "I'm sorry we didn't get to discuss Annie. Seems like you two are getting along well."

"We are. I never thought I could be this happy with anyone. And every day, we seem to get even better."

"That's great to hear. Gives me hope that maybe there's someone out there for me."

Wait. He wasn't going down that road again, was he?

They said their goodbyes and parted. Wyatt would have liked to know about Annie and Caleb. Guess he would just have to see for himself how relationships worked, including business ones.

Chapter 10

Several days had passed since Sierra had seen Wyatt. He was on her mind as she let Fair Creek State Bank's heavy glass door shut behind her and took a wobbly step on the high-heeled shoes she'd scrounged from her closet to impress the bank president. It had been a horrendous morning. No wardrobe sacrifice would have been too much if it helped her get an extension on Aunt Lucy's loan. She wasn't that out of practice wearing heels, but her knees were wobbly, too, from her failed encounter with said bank president.

She took another step and thought she might tumble over onto the sidewalk. A quick glance to see if anyone had noticed her clumsiness revealed a typical weekday afternoon on Fair Creek's Main Street. The sidewalks were all but deserted. The potted petunias on every sidewalk corner sang the praises of the

Fair Creek Garden Club.

She bent down in her tight skirt, managing more like a shimmy, then took off her heels and whirled around to walk barefoot toward Delaney's. Maybe she'd better lay off the ice cream if that had caused the altered fit. But tossing the too-snug skirt to the Fair Creek Thrift Store sounded like a better idea. She loved her ice cream.

She had planned to go back home and change before going to work. But the meeting had lasted longer than she expected. The results were much worse, too. She let the shoes dangle from the fingers on one hand, consumed by a physical need to see her business that took precedence over ditching the uncomfortable clothes. Her bare toes gripped the warm, rough pavement and she drank in the quaint little town. Warmth ran through her at the two rows of flags on each side of the street, one in front of every store.

Things might be dire when it came to the diner's finances. Seeing Wyatt again had brought mixed emotions. But if she'd learned anything through heartaches, it was that the beauty of God's world sometimes came through the most in her worst times.

Thank you, Lord, that you are trustworthy.

Unfortunately, the few extra days she'd been given to make good on the loan wouldn't help much. The one hundred thousand dollars she needed might as well have been a million. Her brain told her the numbers were stacked against her but her heart wouldn't let her give up. Plus, the president had suggested she go to a personal finance support group, like she'd created the debts herself.

Arriving at Delaney's, a renewed fondness for the place welled up in her chest. The aroma of pickles and French fries wafted to her nose from the screened-in back door, used in the summers to combat the heat from the grill.

Annie's questioning look and eyes bright with anticipation nearly undid her. "Didn't expect you back so soon." She blinked and took in a breath. Handling her own disappointment was hard enough but Sierra hated to let others down.

"I got an extension—"

"Oh good, I knew you would!" Annie interrupted before she could finish. Arms went around her for a hug. She welcomed the gesture, turning her head so the close contact didn't make her hearing aids squeal.

Her cousin went right on, not giving her a chance to explain. "Even penny-pinching Mr. Peterson wouldn't want Fair Creek's oldest, friendliest business to go under."

Sierra checked the customer window to be sure no one would overhear her. "I was given until the end of the month to come up with the money."

Her cousin's expression settled into a frown.

"Oh, Sierra! What are you going to do?" Her voice wavered.

If she only knew the answer to that one. An overwhelming sense of her losses hit her, with the reality that the bank really could take her business, the largest tangible evidence left of her family.

"I don't know but I'm not going down without a fight. I mean, he did say I'd be in a stronger position if my financials looked better, if I had more money coming in."

She needed an idea of where to get so much money in such a short amount of time. Everything she had, body and soul, was tied up in Delaney's, just like Annie had warned her about. Without it, she was looking at a black hole. She mentally went through the big wigs she'd met in her former job in advertising. Would any of them want to invest in her? Even if they did, there wasn't enough time to put a deal like that together.

Her mind flitted to Wyatt. He wouldn't have money problems. Hey, maybe if she helped him with his business, he would help her. Not that he would give her the money, or even loan it to her. But he might co-sign for her, if he cared about Fair Creek the way he claimed to.

Yeah, right. You're circling each other like two animals, each waiting for the other to let their guard down.

"You'll find a way." Her cousin patted Sierra's shoulder. "You're a go-getter and aren't over the shock that Aunt Lucy signed for a balloon payment yet."

Guilt gnawed at her for not revealing the true state of Aunt Lucy's finances, although she had just discovered the worst of it today. Annie relied on the paycheck to support her and Chloe and had jumped in to help out with the diner.

Sierra worked to control herself from stomping her foot in frustration about her predicament. "I'm wracking my brain for names of the successful entrepreneurs I've been around from that ad job. It taught me $100,000 is chump change for some people. Risk takers who might take a chance on an underdog. Maybe I know someone who knows someone, like that theory of six degrees of separation."

"I wish you had longer to come up with a plan."

While Sierra mentally ran through the possibilities, Annie had hurried off to take care of something. When Annie returned, Sierra looked up. A dribble of water on the floor next to the walk-in freezer drew her attention and she groaned. "Look."

The ancient appliance's next breakdown might be its last, Fair Creek Appliances had said when they were in. Drip. Drip. Drip. She stood up and was transfixed, the knot in her stomach growing larger with each drip that soon created a puddle.

Annie waved a hand in front of her eyes. "I'll investigate. When it rains it pours, so here come the customers. Yay."

She continued to stare at the scene of her next financial challenge and wished she hadn't banned the word "crisis" from her vocabulary. She thought it was overused, in general.

She said to Annie. "No, you cover the customer. I'll take a look at this."

"Not if you're wearing that you won't." Annie pointed to her skirt and heels.

Sierra had forgotten she still wore her bank interview look, for what good it had done her. Resigned, she walked toward the front and her gaze locked with the dark-brown, nearly black eyes of Wyatt Galloway. Her stomach did a little flip. Here was the last person she wanted to see. She fluffed her hair over her ears and plastered a smile on her face.

Wyatt stood at the counter and didn't have to be a mind reader to know Sierra wasn't happy as she approached. But the set of her jaw and her tense expression didn't prevent him from admiring the green blouse made of some silky fabric that matched the color of her eyes. Her hands clenched and unclenched at her sides.

She reached the counter. This wasn't how he had envisioned things going when he'd glimpsed her earlier walking barefoot in the middle of the sidewalk. After meeting with members of his Vortex Clean Energy team he'd flown in from D.C., he wanted to see her about his solar presentation.

As much as he was enjoying the view, his purpose in coming was strictly business, he reminded himself. He was starved so might as well start there.

"How about one of those homemade strawberry shortcakes listed on your specials board?"

"With ice cream?" She used that professional, unemotional tone that could ice his soul. He nodded, thinking how he'd never seen her so frosty that he could remember. She asked, "Whipped cream, too?"

"The works." He gave her a half-hearted smile.

Her shoulders unhitched. Maybe work was her comfort zone. That he could relate to. By the time she rang up his order and collected his money, he'd decided to abandon the idea of asking her once more to sign on to help promote his business. He wanted her to be in the frame of mind to embrace his ideas.

She turned her back to him to make his order. She went through the steps of preparing his dessert with a graceful flair. He enjoyed watching her. He'd been so involved with Max that women had not been on his radar. But being around her was a nice change he could get used to.

She set the shortcake on the counter, its whipped cream in perfect swirls.

Her smile reached her eyes this time. "Here you go." She seemed to enjoy her work and he liked that.

"It's a masterpiece."

She smiled, then returned toward the work area. He grabbed up the spoon and took a bite.

He walked back, sat where he had the last time he visited with her, and took another scoop of the delectable treat. The sugary strawberry hitting his tongue was the closest he was going to get to heaven on earth. He closed his eyes for a few moments, then opened them and took another bite. He repeated the process several times until he opened his eyes and nearly jumped out of his skin. Sierra stood next to his table. Her clean, musky scent, combined with the set of her jaw, put all his senses on alert.

"How is it?"

"This is the best strawberry shortcake I've ever tasted and that includes Italy, where they think they invented ice cream."

Her lips turned up although he could have sworn a tiny muscle in her jaw twitched.

"My aunt worked for years to perfect the shortcake recipe. It's a family secret."

"And rightly so."

Silence hung between them. She must have something on her mind, and he hoped it was good news for him. It took all of his powers of control to wait for her to speak, and she finally did.

"I've decided to take you up on your proposal." Her face scrunched up and her lips pursed like she'd sucked a lemon. She'd always worn her thoughts in her expression and that hadn't changed. Well, he wouldn't have chosen to work with her either, not under these circumstances with their difficult past, but they needed each other.

"Okay." He set his fork down. "Let's hammer out the details."

He waved her to take a seat across from him.

"Aren't you curious about why I changed my mind?"

This arrangement with her helping him could save his plans for solar energy at Galloway Farm and meet the requirements for the will. "I figure you'll tell me if you want me to know. I'm just happy you've agreed to work together. I haven't really earned the right to know your motivations."

He wanted to tell her he would make sure he was a dream to work with and she wouldn't regret her decision. But she might not believe him, which would hurt. He didn't want to analyze why he cared what she thought.

She looked around the empty dining room and perched on the seat, her back straight.

"I was thinking of sort of a ghost advertising campaign

arrangement." She fiddled with a saltshaker. "I'll stay behind the scenes and provide you with the help you need."

"My idea was to co-write whatever we do and put both our names on it."

She frowned. "And if I'm not willing to do that?"

He pictured promotions with just his name on it, like the other advertising he'd done to no good results.

"Both our names have to be there."

"Why?"

Oh brother. Surely, she could guess the reason. Maybe she wanted to hear him say it.

"Because I want the association of someone familiar and well-known to the people of Fair Creek. I don't want to be an outsider bringing an idea and have all their preconceived suspicions come into play. I want acceptance as a local, because just the Galloway name isn't working."

"What if I don't want our names associated with one another? As I've conceded the point that the Letter to the Editor didn't help you. But repairing that isn't worth taking me down with you."

"I've never taken anyone down, as you phrased it, in my life. Think of this as a collaboration and we'll both come out ahead. Working as a team, we'll be unbeatable."

He could almost see the wheels turning behind those intelligent eyes, and concentrated on finishing off his shortcake.

A light came into her eyes and a confident smile played on her lips. "You're on."

He offered her his hand. Touching her skin that was soft and warm made him want to hold on longer than necessary, and he put his other hand on top as well.

"This is the beginning of a beautiful, new relationship that Fair Creek will reap the rewards from," he said.

Was he wrong to hope that he might get some happiness from it too?

Chapter 11

Three days later, Sierra sat in the midst of a table with strawberries in containers, getting ready to hull them. She gave Annie one of two knives.

"Wyatt wasn't kidding when he said we'd be working together," she said. "Today's lunch crowd was a little bigger and I think he'd sent some guys doing contracting over to have lunch. He's also hired me for more catering at the farm."

Annie nodded toward the strawberries, selected a handful and began hulling. "I know he is connected to needing these."

Sierra cut off a strawberry stem, sorted the part to keep and tossed the rest. Annie did the same and they got into a rhythm. But Sierra wasn't precise with her knife and lost half of some strawberries due to that.

When yet another juicy piece of fruit that clung to a stem

sailed into the trash, it caught her cousin's attention. She stopped and studied Sierra. "Do you want to talk about it?"

She ripped off another strawberry top with the knife. "Talk. Everybody wants to talk all of a sudden."

"The way you're hacking on these, you're losing some good product. I'll take a stab at why you've been in a foul mood. Seems to coincide with the time Wyatt came in the first time. Now he's returned. What gives?"

Sierra attacked another strawberry and hummed along with the classic 70s rock 'n' roll tunes playing in the background. She couldn't make out the words, just the beat, even with hearing aids. Hearing issues ran in her family, but mostly when people got older. She hadn't lost all of her hearing by a long shot. It was frustrating when she didn't know what was missing in normal interactions, not only in song lyrics. Just then Gloria Gaynor pumped out "I Will Survive," loud enough for her to recognize.

The music and the message shook the gloom away. "Wyatt and I were good friends, decided to make the junior prom our first date. But after we had dinner, he dropped me off at the red carpet in torrential rain to park his car so my dress wouldn't get drenched. I never saw him again."

She pelted a rotten strawberry into the trash with excessive force. "I heard things, but I'd never been close with his family and had too much pride to ask them. He'd gotten into a big fight with his dad, but nothing added up. Mom had died a couple years before and I was in a fog. We were friends, mostly during school hours or at Delaney's, unless he let me ride a horse at the farm. Still, he could have said something. Anything." Sierra swallowed. Shouldn't she be over this? Maybe Annie was right, and she had withdrawn from social interaction over time, and that had stunted her progress and caused her to dwell on the Wyatt situation more than normal?

Annie's knife slipped from her fingers onto the counter, and she crossed her arms in front of her. "You have unresolved feelings for him."

"Do you think so?" Sierra stood, grabbed a dish towel and whipped her cousin with it on her way to her guests. "Because of that letter with my nickname for him outlining how friends should stay in touch, I might end up helping him get positive exposure on that solar farm everybody loves to hate."

"That's crazy. You help people to a fault. I've told you that. The letter isn't that huge a deal."

A knot formed in Sierra's stomach. If she hadn't helped the advertising firm every chance she got, she wouldn't have gained valuable, useful skills. She'd learned photography, which had so much value on social media. If a charity in town needed a photo for a T-shirt, a mug, or whatever, she brought her talents forward. She helped when it made sense to, not to her own detriment, not as a door mat.

Sierra went to check on the pot roast and potatoes she'd prepared. The dough for the rolls was in a warm place to rise.

She responded over her shoulder since she was on the move. "You don't know what you're saying. My helping people is a win-win."

"Not everybody is worth helping and sometimes, even if they are, you need to conserve your energies for your own priorities. Maybe free up some time to be able to have a social life, now that you have the hearing aids, possibly be in a situation to meet someone."

"The last thing I want, or have time for, is a relationship. I've told you." She fluffed her hair.

"Who said anything about a relationship? How about a date, somebody to have dinner with or go to a movie? Someone to discuss your ideas for boosting sales with." Her cousin brought the last couple quarts of strawberries and set them in between them.

Sierra needed to introduce some balance. "Your past relationships weren't anything to brag about, not until Caleb. But apparently just having a boyfriend who seems pretty great for six months qualifies you to give advice."

"Good point. But I think you're scared."

She wanted to walk away. But Annie acted like this was an important conversation. And maybe it was.

"You know I love you, Sweetie. But I have to say this. Your hearing issues have impacted your life. When your hearing was fading, you started withdrawing, day by day. I saw what was happening. I mean, I was a reporter and we lived in different cities, but we checked in with one another. You didn't pull back from me, necessarily, but we had struggles with phone conversations. Whenever I would ask what you had been doing, you had less to say."

What was this, pick on Sierra day? "And what if I did?" She hadn't meant to sound defensive. "It's natural to eliminate situations where I'm not comfortable. It was gradual and I didn't realize I was doing it."

"Nothing wrong with that, but you're a great person and you have lots to offer. Remember that song we used to sing in Sunday school, *This Little Light of Mine*? Your light wasn't shining. I thought the hearing aids would help but I'm not so sure."

"It's only been a week and it's been hard."

"I believe you. You're no wimp and I have no reason to doubt what you're saying. How can I help?"

"I'll get it figured out."

They finished the rest of the strawberries, and it was nearing time to greet the employees Wyatt had brought in from D.C. He was buying their dinner at Delaney's. She didn't want to analyze anything. Wyatt was fulfilling his part of the deal in better ways than she anticipated. Sierra made a clean break for the dining room before Annie could bring up anything else that made her uncomfortable.

Caleb greeted Wyatt at his front door and he walked into the foyer with Max on his arm. He'd come to take a break from the frenzied pace he'd been working. Ever since Sierra had agreed to collaborate, he'd spent a few days making major headway on his plans. There were still more calls to make and information needed to be distributed.

"Thanks for letting me drop in. I needed the break."

"Quite alright. The more the merrier is my philosophy. It seems like it's a revolving door around here sometimes."

They stepped into the kitchen. Caleb's girlfriend Annie's daughter sat at the dining room table drinking a glass of milk. She was dressed in a full softball uniform, at eight years old.

"Tonight's my softball game."

"Hey, slugger."

Her smile told him she didn't mind the nickname he'd chosen.

"Hi, 'Uncle Wyatt,' oops, I mean Mr. Grumpy, are you coming to my game?"

She'd chosen that nickname for him the first time they met. Maybe the fact that the name didn't bother him that much was part of the problem.

This was all new to him, just dropping by to see family.

Caleb leaned down and looked at Max while he slept. "Seems like he's grown a lot since I saw him last, but it's only been a few days. They say it goes fast and I can see why."

Aunt Elizabeth came from the direction of the living room and entered the kitchen. "Hi, Wyatt." She reached for Max, who was still in his car seat. "Let me take him off your hands?"

"I appreciate the offer but are you sure? I wouldn't want to take advantage. I'm so grateful to you for bringing him home to me sooner by escorting him on the plane."

"That was my pleasure. To answer your question, it's fine. I'm going to be staying here with Drew and Ella while Caleb and

Annie are at the game."

"He may be down for the count and will be fine here. But it's your call."

Something about the fact that Chloe thought he was her uncle sealed the deal. He turned to Elizabeth, "Yes, please tuck Max in. I'm going to see this girl play ball."

"Yay!" The child who wanted to be his niece jumped around the room. His face might have turned a bit red from the response, but it was nice to be recognized, too.

The game would start soon so Max was put in the playpen that could be made into a crib. Wyatt looked in on him beside his sleeping niece and nephew, and then tip toed out.

On the ride over, Caleb offered to catch them up on the lawyer meeting.

Caleb informed everyone that Kayla, the only Galloway sister and Drew and Ella's mom, had relapsed in drug rehab. He felt sad for Kayla, for all of them really, but Wyatt's loyalty was to his niece and nephew. They were innocents.

Caleb had said very little. "What's the deal, Caleb? You trying to replace me as Mr. Grump?"

Chloe gave him a toothy grin. "He can be Mr. Grump Two."

Annie, sitting next to her, handed her some earbuds. "Honey, I don't want you too worked up before the game. Why don't you listen to your music?"

Annie turned to Wyatt. "Caleb's having a hard time with some things, including your dad's death."

Was this something else on Caleb's mind the other night, that the babies' needs had caused him to put on hold? Wyatt wanted to handle this just right. The rest of them were closer to John Galloway than he had been. "Death is always hard." *Way to state the obvious.* Although some deaths were harder than others.

Caleb grunted.

"He was there when your dad had his heart episode," Annie said.

Like he didn't know that? Maybe reassurance was in order. "Yes, and I heard the ambulance got there in record time."

Chapter 12

The adults seemed to think about John's passing, and what he had meant to them. They rode a little while in silence.

"Here's what I can't get out of my head," Caleb said. "I was discussing a land deal with Dad around the time when he started having problems. I knew he was unhappy about my idea, of me and my California buddies investing in the farm. I thought if he understood more about our plans, he might go for it."

If Caleb thought he had contributed to Dad's death, that would be a reason he'd lost a bit of his lightheartedness.

Wyatt cleared his throat. "I can understand how you would feel, especially if he got really upset," he said. "But there is a lot we don't know about people's health and how their bodies work. Heart attacks have a genetic component. Grandpa Galloway died of a heart attack, when we were little."

Caleb responded from the driver's seat. "When you put it like that, I see what you mean. Guess I'm having an emotional reaction that might not be based in reality."

Annie chimed in. "Kayla's addiction and the twins coming to live with you really upset him. I was there and I remember well. That's a day I'll never forget and will always cherish, so I've put John's reaction out of my mind. He wasn't happy though. I don't know that he talked about it with anybody, just kept it inside, would be my guess."

Caleb turned off the radio. "I'm sure you're right. Thanks. He knew I wasn't going to pressure him into anything. I am hanging on to that."

Annie said, "You have nothing to feel guilty about. And remember that our number of days on earth are in God's hands. Your dad wouldn't want you feeling this way."

"There's my team! Mommy, let's go!"

Caleb pulled into the field at the ballpark where everyone parked and Annie went to check Chloe in with her team that she'd spotted in a side field warming up.

The truck ride had left Wyatt a bit raw, talking about Dad's death. He wasn't used to such open conversations and talking about emotional situations. The way Annie soothed Caleb's concerns had touched him and wasn't similar to anything he'd ever experienced in a relationship.

It made him want to see Sierra. She was at the concessions area and he was going to go find her. Stopping to analyze why didn't appeal to him.

Chapter 13

Sierra slung the gallon of ice cream into the Fair Creek summer league's dilapidated freezer and shoved the door closed. The appliance needed replaced and she hoped it would hold out in this sweltering heat. She couldn't contain her excitement. Tonight, for the first time, she'd be selling ice cream at the Fair Creek concession. She concentrated on arranging the plastic bowls and napkins just so.

"Wow, these ball fields used to seem so spacious. Not anymore." At the sound of Wyatt's voice, butterflies summersaulted in her stomach. What was he doing here?

She whirled around to find him resting his forearms on the other side of the counter. Wyatt's cowboy hat was tilted just right and his broad grin with straight white teeth about did her in. A black T-shirt showed off muscular pecs. Her mouth fell open and she closed it. She inhaled his woodsy scent, and her night had just turned even more perfect.

She fluffed the hair down around her ears and beamed him a smile. "You dress down well." *So much for sticking to business.*

He grinned. "Thanks, I think." His smile warmed her heart.

Silence stretched out between them. He seemed as tongue-tied as she felt. The glint in his eyes made her wonder if he might have some of the same feelings she did. She might have been interested in exploring her mixed emotions, if there wasn't so much going on in her life right now. She swallowed and got back on track. "I know what you meant. The ball fields seemed huge when we were young, didn't they? When Annie used to hit a homerun over the fence, I felt like that ball was in the air forever."

"You would know all about that."

She smiled that he remembered she'd been Annie's biggest cheerleader during softball season. "True." She shrugged. "A lot of what we believed as kids didn't turn out to be true, did it?"

He held up his large hand, the long fingers splayed. "Let's not get too deep."

Oh, you're wrong. That's exactly what I need, a real conversation.

She grinned and made a production of locating her bag of plastic spoons, then shoved a handful into a container. "What is deep to one person is shallow to someone else. But I came to sell ice cream, not debate Shakespeare."

"So, I'm curious, how long have you been setting up shop here? How many games a week?"

She breathed in. Business conversation represented solid

ground, and she pulled her gaze from him in his new jeans and swallowed. "If all goes well, it'll be two nights a week."

"Seems like a good idea. I don't know why it wouldn't be five."

She didn't care what he thought, with his business likely having endless employees who could probably cover two locations, or fifty. "We'll see. A local college intern conducted a customer traffic study for us. On Delaney's lightest customer days in the summer, the whole town was out at the ballpark."

"Seems like a smart thing to do." His eyes shone with admiration, for her business talents, she assumed. *Don't let yourself hope there is maybe something else too.* "That's a money-savvy move, too, cutting out an expense of hiring a marketing firm. Showing up in the community."

"Aunt Lucy was a master at stretching money. She had no choice. Whenever she involved students, they took an interest in the business, hanging around and bringing their friends, which boosted our customer numbers." That's why her digging such a hole in the end was so painful.

He nodded. "From experience, even if you do spend top dollar on marketing advice, that won't always result in more sales."

"We discovered that at the ad agency I worked for, too."

He lifted his cowboy hat and ran his fingers through his hair, the humidity must have made it more curly. She'd touched his hair once when checking him for a fever. Once had gone a long way at the time. She'd had dreams about it afterwards. She looked down at the spoons she'd put in wrong and rearranged them. Sierra glanced outside where people were crowded around the diamonds watching. Hopefully, they'd be coming her way, or this experiment would be a bust. Fans sat on bleachers or their own travel chairs while others stood along the fences near the dugouts.

After a while, a man about her age approached the counter. "Hey, one of the guys has a birthday today," he said. "We're going to celebrate right here."

"Party Central at your service." She grinned. His dark hair and brown eyes registered somewhere in her memory. Fair Creek's population of about 3,000 people meant she didn't know every single one of them. A moment later, she recognized him as a volunteer from the fire department who had collected money for the new fire truck. He placed his order and she started humming.

This could be good. The volunteer firemen's baseball team might have more than the typical nine players to serve. Just one team would be a boost in her customer numbers. Looking for Wyatt, she spotted him leaning against a nearby tree, so he must have left when she was busy. His muscular forearms folded across his chest caught her attention and he was looking toward the game being played.

One by one the firemen came up to the counter and ordered. She dipped ice cream and topped off each one with syrup, whipped cream from the can and a maraschino cherry.

After a while, her wrist was tired and perspiration trickled down her back. She swiped her arm across her forehead, certain she had taken care of two entire teams by now. But the line had gotten longer, not shorter. Wyatt stood near the tree but he'd told her earlier Chloe's game had ended and she won. He'd stopped watching the games and observed Sierra instead.

That flutter in her stomach took hold again but she focused on work.

Someone beside her grazed her elbow. "You need help here." She'd been too busy to notice Annie had come in. "Wish I could stay but we're celebrating Chloe's game."

"I'll kick you out if you try. Now, go."

"Oh, and Wyatt wants to stick around. He came with us. Will you give him a ride home? He said it's okay with him, if you approve."

Sierra's gaze wandered to Wyatt. No longer even pretending an interest in the games, he watched her intently if a little bit stiff, like he might be on edge about something. He cared, about what, she wasn't sure. This was the first she'd heard about giving him a ride. She wasn't thrilled about it but couldn't pinpoint what to say.

"Of course, I'll give him a ride. No problem. What about Max?"

"You sure? The games got off schedule and Elizabeth agreed to stay late and take care of him and the twins."

"I'm sure. Now go give Chloe an extra hug for me and enjoy yourselves."

More customers had come as games ended and others started. She looked up and saw women in uniforms, members of a powerhouse softball team that played late at night.

Wyatt's shoulder that rested against tree bark started to get uncomfortable. His gaze remained fixed on Sierra, much more interesting than any game. He shoved himself away from the tree and stretched.

Clusters of people waited for ice cream with no sign of letting up, and she worked alone. But judging by the glow of her skin and her bright smile, she seemed to be in her element. And being a little shop, maybe she didn't have anyone to call.

Men in his age-range continued to parade to the counter to buy ice cream. Most were rough around the edges, with dusty jeans and scruffy beards. Yet she offered a smile to everyone. He dug the toe of his shoe into the ground, folded and refolded his arms. There were some women customers too. The more times men stepped up, though, the more irritated he became. He couldn't explain a logical reason for it.

Maybe Chloe's right about your being Mr. Grumpy.

He must be jealous, which was unusual for him. The desire to be near her occupied him. His feet propelled him toward the tiny building where she worked. He had no idea what he would do when he got there. Get in line to buy ice cream?

Before he could talk himself out of it, he had reached the structure, turned the doorknob, and stepped inside. Sierra took orders at the counter with her back to him. He had no idea what he would say when she turned around, how to explain his being there. Scents of chocolate and strawberries mixed with too many people in a hot place hung in the air. His gaze landed on an apron that poked out of a bag hanging on a hook. Yanking the apron out of the bag, he managed to tie the strings into a sloppy knot before she noticed him.

Head down, Sierra turned around and dipped into the ice cream. She looked up and jumped. Wyatt stood next to her, wearing an apron. The Delaney's letters were rumpled from when she wadded it up in her bag. But no one had ever looked better to her. Sparkling eyes the shade of cold brew coffee and a perfect row of white teeth, with a dimpled grin greeted her. Her heart twisted.

This would never do.

"Why are you here?"

"I'd like to help you," he said. "Now, where's an extra scoop?"

She went and found a scoop. But what if he came too near her ears?

But once properly equipped, he got down to business filling one of her orders. The muscles in his arm flexed as he scooped a dip of the frozen ice cream more quickly than she could have.

To keep her mind off Wyatt, she focused on business too. She didn't want to raise prices so she needed to sell more. One of the college marketing classes had proved that a high quantity of sales could make up for selling fewer units at higher prices, in theory, anyway.

In the tiny space, he stood out in jeans just as much as he would in a suit. Maybe he really couldn't help getting noticed. She grabbed the nearest paper, which was a stray list of kids on a Little League team, and fanned herself. It didn't help that the July heatwave had arrived.

Or maybe having that extra body in here was overheating her. Staying out of one another's way proved impossible, too. Their hands collided, and shoulders brushed as they filled the orders.

Stray whipped cream ended up on her nose. When Wyatt brushed the white fluff away, his intense dark eyes were so, so close. There were those gold flecks of his again. The muggy night was getting to both of them, and they used the clean towels for swiping off, when they had the chance.

The rush ended as fast as it had started. They leaned against the deep freeze of ice cream bars to catch their breath.

"My marketing idea worked!"

He smiled and looked out toward the ball field. "Here comes another team."

She couldn't think of anything more fun than working with him and making money, too. Something beeped in her ear. Her hearing aid was warning her the battery would go dead. Great. The restrooms were far away across the park. This was new and she carried spares in her purse like she'd been advised to do. But she didn't want to replace the batteries in public, especially her first time. She eyed the line. She'd taken in so much new information when she got them. She couldn't remember how much time if would be until the battery went dead, and they'd actually said it could vary.

She continued to work, hoping for the best. With a last beep, the sound in her left ear went dull, like a lamplight blowing out. The next few words someone spoke were a bit muffled. Just like that, she struggled to make out what people were saying. She pushed on, straining to hear their orders.

Her mind warred with herself while she worked, making things worse. Why did she have to be secretive? Being vain wasn't a good trait to have and maybe she needed to reconsider practicality over vanity.

Ted Mitchell stepped up with his great-grandson. "It's nice to see Delaney's out here. What a great idea." He spoke louder than normal, maybe because he was at the ballpark and excited. She did some lip reading to understand him.

"Good to see you in a different setting, Ted." Whatever he said next might have been small talk. She simply nodded, hoping she wasn't agreeing to participate in an armed robbery or donate more money than she had to charity or something.

'We'll take two chocolate ice cream cones." She'd watched his lips closely and felt sure she'd gotten the order correct. Using "visual cues," as her audiologist called it, she could see there were two of them so it made sense.

Trotting back to make the cones, she squelched a big yawn. She checked the wall clock. It showed almost seven forty-five. The chocolate ice cream was just about out. A quick check showed all of the flavors were low.

Bringing the cones to Ted and his great grandchild, she handed them over and named the price. They both just looked at her.

The boy's sweet smile didn't leave his face but he shouted, "Where's my pop?"

So she *had* missed something, the drink order. She plastered on a smile. "Coming right up!"

Catching up to Wyatt, she said, "Looks like we're about to run out of ice cream. What a fantastic night. I'm thrilled. I don't think anyone's going to mind that I'm shutting down before the games are over."

He shrugged. "What else can you do? Maybe it'll teach them to come earlier next time."

"That reminds me, I'd like to put a sign up with when I'm coming next. You've been so great about everything. Would you mind making something simple while I gather things up? The supplies are over there."

After getting what he needed, he went outside to a picnic table to design her announcement.

Since no customers were around, she crept underneath the counter and replaced both hearing aid batteries, which she'd been told kept them working at peak performance.

Maybe she could be grateful for the hearing aids, even if she wasn't ready to shout out that she had them. Not yet anyway.

Her prayers had been partially answered, with a new mental attitude gradually evolving about her situation. She'd take it as a step forward.

Only those closest to her knew about them. Since Wyatt wouldn't become close, she wanted to spare them both the discomfort she knew would follow when he found out. She hadn't adjusted to her situation well. How could she expect him to?

At eight, she pulled down the cover that closed the concession stand window. What else would Wyatt help her with? She couldn't wait to find out.

Chapter 14

Sierra didn't really want Wyatt helping her clean the Fair Creek Park concession stand but he insisted. "It'll go extra fast with two," he said.

When they finished and exited the booth, whooping and hollering from a distant ball field greeted them. Sierra blinked at the stars that twinkled overhead in the night sky. They headed toward the sound. Her athletic shoes were no match for the clumped grass under her feet and the rough terrain. She nearly fell in the dark but caught herself just in time.

"My brothers and I have season tickets at pro ballparks across the country. All the fancy boxes and perks can't compete with this fresh country air, the local rivalries." He paused. "Or the company I'm with."

It was a sweet thing to say, except something about him

sounding all sentimental like that irritated Sierra. It didn't help that some body parts ached, like a prizefighter might feel after a few rounds. She had dipped a lot of ice cream in a short time.

"Reality check here. You left this in a heartbeat without looking back. The small-town charm will lose interest for you. We'll still be here."

I'll still be here–without you.

"Wow. I get that it wasn't good how we parted. But you make it sound like you've never left. How long were you gone, anyway?"

"I've thought about this over the past few days. If it hadn't been such a rough time in my life, I'm pretty sure what happened wouldn't have been such a big deal. My mother dying tore my heart out and you were like another loss. To answer your question, I won't count college, since I was home every summer. I was eleven years at the ad agency. How do you know so much about my career?"

"I don't. But you know how you get some downtime you didn't plan on, and for a few minutes, you think about old friends and look for somebody online?"

"At least you thought about me long enough to do a Google search. Hey, I think that's got potential as a country song lyric. What do you think?"

He laughed and put his arm around her shoulder before removing it rather quickly. "What I think is, these conversations that we used to have are what I've really missed about you. There was a space in my life that no one else could fill. Don't assume that because you didn't hear from me, I wasn't missing you."

Sierra swallowed a lump in her throat. There was still a lot she didn't know but this, these words, did a lot to heal her heart.

"I am at a loss to say something that eloquent. I've really missed you too."

On the field, the catcher smashed into the fence trying to catch a pop foul. The ball flew behind the backstop and slammed onto the paved parking lot among some parked cars.

"I'd better get that before it's lost," she said. "Balls and equipment are expensive. The kids have gone on home."

"Let me. You've put in a long—"

"I need to get the kinks out after all of that bending and dipping. Race you to that park bench over by where it landed?"

"You're on!"

She judged that she would get there ahead of him, just barely. But winning didn't matter like it might have if he hadn't just said the most amazing thing to her.

Her foot landed in a hole and she lurched to the side. One shoulder collided with him and his six-pack abs. She tried to correct her trajectory, but momentum brought him down with her. She landed partly on top of him. Strong, warm arms enveloped her.

"Are you alright?"

She leaned her head away so the hearing aids wouldn't whistle, glad it was dark so he couldn't see them.

"As long as there isn't a raccoon like last time you had your arms around me. I don't know how I'm going to get over that. Might need an intervention." He felt good to be near, like her protector.

He's left before. What's to stop him from leaving again?

"I'm sorry for letting you down. That was a part of what I dealt with."

She couldn't allow herself to get comfortable this way, he was like coming home for her. After a few moments, she pulled away. He stayed close to support her, held her elbow to steady her. When he let his hand drop, and they weren't touching, she missed him.

Just keep it cool, nothing heavy.

She gulped some air. "Sorry about that, didn't mean to fall on you," she said, forcing a casual tone while she brushed herself off.

She faced him. "It's really nice now to be valued for the friendship we shared. But what happened? I don't want to belabor the point because it's pretty old news. How about giving me the condensed version?"

"Dad and I had been butting heads for a long time. You knew that. At prom, I was parking the car in torrential rain so you wouldn't get your dress wet when he came across me on the street. It wasn't so much different from any other confrontation we'd had, looking back on it. There was nothing I ever did that was right by him. So when he stopped and started yelling at me for equipment I had left out in the barn, and other miscellaneous complaints, things I'd done so I could go to prom, I couldn't take it anymore. I left that night. I left you. Even though we were just friends, I did owe you an explanation."

"You had been impulsive. I knew about how you struggled

with your dad. I just didn't think it would come to that."

"I was a kid, self-centered. Angry and not sure even why. Everything had fallen apart."

She searched for words and turned on her cell phone flashlight to wave across the ground searching for that ball. She needed to offset the intensity of this conversation "You know how people love their police scanners. We knew you and your dad had gotten physical and a cop separated you. There was speculation that, because of your family, details about how bad it was were exaggerated. It was like you crashed your own world, sounds like."

"Guess I didn't see it that way. Sure didn't seem like a choice at the time. I realize I'm not the first kid to fight with their dad. The whole thing sounds pretty lame, almost like a cliché. He never liked anything I did and things were only going to get worse. That's how it looked to me, at eighteen-years-old."

"I know you'd talked about the problems. I just didn't know you'd dump me out, too. We were close. And maybe getting closer, at least we'd talked about it."

"I wasn't good enough for you anymore, if I ever had been. I felt like a failure. I had too much pride to come back and didn't want to, honestly."

Now she remembered. For a kid with as much money as the Galloways had, he had never felt worthy. But what a ridiculous statement.

Spotting the blasted ball they were hunting, she stomped over and snatched the firm shape from a clump of grass. "You should have let me decide that."

"Like I really needed to add rejection onto the rest I was going through."

The small crowd of the last devoted fans behind them started booing, about an official's call, she assumed. This conversation was going so differently than she thought it would.

"You knew that we were our own twosome and I couldn't reach out to your family. I'd lost my mom and was never that confident around adults. People talked at school but I relied on you to contact me and you never did. I wouldn't have rejected you."

"That's easy to say. You were always judgmental."

She stumbled on words to explain. "You've made me sound like an awful person." He wasn't making sense. "Moving away like that must have impacted your thinking? I have expectations and want people to be the best they can be, pretty normal stuff."

"Ironically, the only reason we're talking now is because you criticized me in the paper."

She gulped in a huge breath and huffed it out. "It wasn't supposed to be..."

She walked around, so bothered by what he said that she couldn't stand still. When she stopped and looked into his eyes, the pain was there. "We were kids and just doing normal kid jokes, never hurt anybody. We did the fundraisers for children's hospitals together even. I'm not proud of what you're bringing up though and won't defend it. I think it was my own insecurities."

"Maybe I can see that now. I didn't have the perspective then."

"Friends stick together. I could have helped, offered moral support, if you'd given me the chance."

She turned away from him. There had been talk at school, everywhere, and the more time went that he hadn't answered her, the less she had defended him. At that age, a few months seemed like a year and she'd definitely moved on and that's when she and Shirley had gotten close and she'd finished out a great school year, actually.

The knot in her stomach signaled that he might have more to share. She wasn't sure if she was ready for it.

Chapter 15

Standing out in the dark at Fair Creek Park, Wyatt could sense how stricken Sierra was. "Look, I don't want to get carried away. I never wanted to hurt you."

In some strange way, he felt closer to her, for giving him this chance to sort through his past. She had always demanded more from him than anyone ever had. No one ever pressed him the way she had. He wasn't sure if he missed it or not. He did know that he felt more alive than he had in months, maybe years.

He joined her with pacing the parking lot. "I'm not saying I was rational. You were never mean. Still aren't. I was up against the wall when I left and focused on survival. I had to grow up fast."

Some of the stiffness in the way she held her body seemed to lessen right before his eyes. Her shoulders relaxed. "A million things went through my head when I didn't hear from you."

He should go away and just leave her alone. What was the point of this?

"Look. It's okay. You sure were harder on yourself than you ever were on anyone else. Like what did you think?"

Wyatt followed her gaze. The partial moon shone bright. Stars that looked like tiny pin pricks twinkled in the clear night sky.

She shrugged and giggled nervously. "Kidnappings and stuff. You know I read a lot and was always in my head. I was young, naïve, and obsessed over too many novels, I guess? Plus, I didn't believe you would ignore texts, not after what you meant to me."

"When I wasn't coming back, my parents shut off my phone. I had my own money from summer jobs and could pay for places to stay. After several days, maybe a week, I decided to head to D.C. since my distant cousin, Miles, lived there. Where would we be without family reunions to meet distant cousins who live out of state?"

He snickered, "It sounds like an excuse but we were both young and I know I was immature. The first thing his parents did was let mine know where I was. I would imagine their pride kept them from sharing details. I'd decided you were better off without me. I can't blame it on you. I didn't want anyone to try to talk me into coming back."

"My self-esteem was so low, I believed everyone was glad I was gone. I was trying to survive at the same time I figured out how to make a life. In finishing out school at his high school, he and I were into all kinds of things, which included solar energy. It's how we started Vortex Clean Energy. When he didn't go through with it after graduation, I became sole owner."

She reached out to him then. They hugged, just stood together with their arms around each other. She sniffled into his shirt. It was a short, comforting embrace and then they separated.

But it was long enough for him to know they fit one another, almost like she was his missing piece.

A bat cracked on a ball somewhere and he shook his head.

She lifted her hands to her ears and fluffed her hair. Really, what *was* it with her?

Although, he'd just run his fingers through his own hair. It was a habit with him. She still didn't say anything, but scuffed one toe into the ground.

"Guess the short version went long. Anyway, I hope you can forgive me and I appreciate how you're working with me on ways for the community to accept me, a little better, at least. I've never been in a position where I'm proposing ideas for the place where I live."

They walked along slowly, like they were both worn out. He loosely put his arm around her shoulder. She didn't lean in but didn't shrug him off either.

With her chin up, and her steel-eyed gaze on him, so close it penetrated the dark, he could almost believe she saw right through him.

"When I told you I'd help, I meant it."

"Thanks for brushing off the skills you used at the advertising agency for me. You're the best. After that Stallion remark, I'm going to need an air-tight plan like only you can create."

He fluttered his T-shirt away from his body where humidity held it there like glue, or maybe he'd been sweating bullets with that conversation he didn't want to repeat anytime soon.

He said, "Don't go beating yourself up. I mean, you started an economic growth council where there's barely an economy."

She laughed.

"I will never forget this night. That's for sure," he said.

She gave him a half grin as they returned the ball to the last straggling umpire, loading equipment into his trunk. His explanation to Sierra, as unsatisfying as it was even to his ears, made him feel like a weight had been lifted. Maybe they'd returned to their old friendly footing, hopefully. He wondered if they really had returned to that or if this might be something different, something new, something better.

No sooner had she handed the ball over to the official and headed toward the van with Wyatt than huge raindrops started pelting her cheeks. *Saved by the rain.*

Good timing, or bad? She didn't know which. At least she was closer to putting some distance between them. That conversation had been brutal and what Wyatt had said about her still stung, let alone his explanation for why her messages to him had gone unanswered.

Cool raindrops were welcome relief on her skin as she lifted her face to the sky. Indiana was known for quick weather changes, but this turnaround from savage heat to thunderstorm seemed like a record.

Wyatt leaned down to her level. "You always loved rain."

He was right. And it thrilled her that he remembered. All the muscles in her body relaxed. So, what was the anxiety in her gut? Oh yeah. A small panic overtook her. Her hearing aids couldn't get wet. There were apparently some hearing aids that were waterproof, but they cost more. *I mean, probably a few drops wouldn't be a problem, and hair would catch some moisture.*

As if a cloud had burst open, rain came in waves across the sky, with no letting up. This was no gentle rain. With no time to explain, she had to run to shelter to stay dry. She tore away from him across the park toward her van at the back of the lot, hit the key fob, and scrambled in. After putting the key in the engine, she turned the air conditioner on low.

Seconds later, Wyatt opened the passenger door and slid into the seat beside her. Water dripped off of him onto the seat. "I didn't know you could run so fast." He removed his cowboy hat and set it on his lap. They'd turned off the ball field lights. The two of them were surrounded by darkness, with rain streaming down the windshield, like they were in a cocoon.

Her stomach did a little twist. Even soaking wet he was drop-dead gorgeous.

"I just wanted to dodge some rain."

The close quarters increased the level of intimacy swirling

around them. "Since we used to play in the rain and not care about getting wet, I was surprised when you ran. But why should I be? Maybe I've hung onto the way things were more than I should have. Sorry."

"I'm as guilty as you are of assuming you've stayed the same, and thinking I know you. It's probably normal since we got along so well and were inseparable."

He had always been easy to talk to and that hadn't changed. Wyatt said, "You were a big part of my life, and we went through significant stages together."

His words soothed her. Maybe what she'd wanted all along was to know that their time together had mattered to him. "It's good to hear you say that. We were at such an important age in life, too. Not to dwell on Mom's death, but losing her ended my childhood, I feel like. Maybe it makes sense we'd make a lasting impression on one another."

Since he'd shared about what he'd been through, it was hard to hang onto her anger toward him. Forgiving him might come harder. Nobody came away unscathed in the process of living, and she wouldn't trade places with what he'd been through for anything.

A thunderclap startled them both. Lightning streaked the sky. Her phone beeped with a text.

The Fair Creek warning system said a severe weather alert had been issued through 4 a.m. Tornadoes had been spotted in several counties, including Leigh County. The power in town was out.

Sierra groaned.

"I better subscribe to that messaging system." Wyatt looked at his phone. "But Galloway Farm isn't normally without power when the town is. We'd hook up a generator anyway. When you drop me off, it's no problem if you want to clean up at my place. I know I'm feeling pretty sticky from working in that small, hot space. And no offense, but unless you have a great place in town, which is full of pretty old houses that won't do you much good in high winds, I'd rather you spend the night."

She didn't know if she was ready for that. Maybe shift to a safe topic now. "Selling all that ice cream was definitely the high point of the night for me."

"I can relate. Some people just don't get how much fun competing in business can be. The extra-curriculars you and I did together in school must have prepared us for entrepreneurship."

She really wanted to go home, but not to a hot apartment without power. She was grungy and had to have a shower before she'd be able to sleep. "Well, if you're sure I wouldn't be imposing on you."

Something in her was shattered by his revelations though. Exhaling a breath, she took the van out of park and headed toward the farm. Taking things too seriously had been a problem for her as long as she could remember, and this had been a rough night. Aunt Lucy had always told her to lighten up, but how could she?

Wyatt picked up his hat and spun it on his finger. "It's like starting over, isn't it? We know each other, but we really don't."

Out of the corner of her eye, she glanced at his handsome

profile and her heart skidded in her chest.

She said, "It's like we skipped the chit chat, getting-to-know you part. Honestly, that was heavy back there and I can't take more of that, tonight." Maybe not ever but she wasn't going to share that.

"Boy, I second that. Remembering that stuff was harder on me than I thought. I'm still upset if I think about it."

Sierra liked driving and being in control, which relaxed her. The rain had all but stopped. "Then let's not. Going to the ballpark reminded me of Aunt Lucy. She would let me leave early from the diner for Annie's ballgames. We had a ritual at the end of the day, really just a conversation starter." She ran out of air and ended on a tight sob. Grief could sneak up on a person.

"She was a gem, your aunt was." Respect laced the observation along with a fond smile. "I blame her for my ice cream addiction. Let's hear what you used to do."

His calm and reassuring voice helped ease the memories and she'd pulled herself together. "Ask questions that brought answers that made us happy, basically."

The van's interior didn't seem as big with Wyatt inside and his knee seemed so near, almost touching hers. He was a steady presence.

She only hoped they didn't have a tornado in their future.

Chapter 16

As she drove, Sierra tried to prepare herself to go into his house. They'd be getting to the farm soon so she needed to step things up, to "elevate the mood," an Aunt Lucy phrase. "So what is the best thing that's ever happened to you?"

Without hesitation, he answered in a tone of awe. "The night Max was born. Having a son has topped everything else. It's made up for anything difficult that's occurred. Maybe that I will ever go through."

He thumped his hat against one knee. "What about you?"

Sierra swallowed, and engaged her turning signal. She didn't have a baby of her own, had figured romance and motherhood would pass her by. But his story lowered her defenses, making her long for more.

"Mine would be two things and I'm torn. Once my mom

made a black raspberry pie for Grandpa, her dad. It was one of those exceptional days for no real reason. I can still picture them together in my mind in his kitchen, although they've been gone for years. Mom made crusts from scratch and I can see the sugar she sprinkled on the top layer like it was sitting in front of me right now, and can taste the berries. They were together and he raved over her cooking. It's why I feature black raspberry pies at the store so often."

She turned into the farm's long drive, and in the distance, the huge, imposing arch came into view. "Mine was *really* too long. Look, we're almost to your place."

Wyatt asked, "What's your second thing? Since you're doing two, the second one has to be one sentence, no more than ten words."

"Hey, don't try to take over my game."

"The clock is ticking."

She was almost to the house. She tapped off the number of words with her fingers on the steering wheel as she said them. "The day Annie and Chloe moved upstairs above Delaney's. Family."

He threw his head back and laughed. The sound was like nobody else's. "You did it! I'm not going to take off points for the one lone word at the end."

She was more pleased by his reaction than she should have been. He didn't find that many things laugh-out-loud funny, at least he hadn't in the past.

If only her nerves weren't going a little haywire. She was a mess, and it would have been dumb not to take him up on his offer. She had a lot to do tomorrow and needed to get a good night's sleep. But she worried about how well this was all going to go.

He put his hand over hers, and her stomach fluttered. But he pulled away immediately. "We did have some fun times, didn't we? I never intended for what happened to go down the way it did."

He looked out at the eery sky, silent after the thunderstorm. "I'll be surprised if the area avoids a tornado touch down tonight. It's good you're staying here tonight, even though you'd probably rather go home."

"Well, I live on the third floor of Beeson Place, that old music conservatory they turned into apartments. So, I'll be taking you up on your offer and grateful for it."

She could just make out the large cabin style house, which looked more imposing in the dark.

"You look a little spooked. Being in the country at night can be nerve wracking if you're not used to it. Just stay there."

He hopped out of the vehicle, and while he went around the van to open her door, she made a mental checklist of what she needed for the night. There wasn't anything in the van that needed to go in the house. She grabbed her bag.

When he took her hand to lead the way, that feeling of being protected came over her again. "I could get used to this," she said. Wyatt had barely turned the knob and ushered her in when toenails clicked on the hardwood floors and a medium-sized brown dog trotted up. The mutt sniffed her.

"I didn't figure you for a dog person."

"Sadie here didn't get the memo. Showed up outside a couple nights ago, looking starved. A leftover hamburger from the grill bonded us for life. She's house trained. I've got to figure she was abandoned, which people do a lot out here." He leaned down and stroked the dog's small, pointed ear, and she exhaled a low moan. "An ear massage put me into her eternal graces."

Moving out of the entry way, the living room's dark, stained wood walls seemed like a sanctuary now, given the weather. The cozy setting was loosening her defenses. The loveseat with a crocheted throw over the back called to her to snuggle up. If she reached for his hand, pulled him over there, would he wrap those big, strong arms around her again?

You better snap out of it, girl.

Coming here had been a terrible idea, not from a safety perspective but from a personal-space angle, if she wanted to keep her distance. But she focused on tamping down her neediness and allowed herself to be ushered into the large room, with Sadie following.

"Let me take you back where you can clean up for the night."

He stepped into a hallway, and she followed, Sadie their silent companion at every move. They reached a door and Wyatt opened it. "Here's the guest bedroom and there's a bathroom with a shower, should be everything you need."

A patchwork quilt covered the queen-sized bed, with a stool that served as a nightstand that had been stacked high with hardback books, and an upholstered chair in one corner.

He walked in, opened the closet door, and she could see rows of shirts. He really had a large wardrobe but nothing for a cowboy. Coming out with a dress shirt, he handed it to Sierra.

"This is my spare closet. Here, take this with you to wear. Everything you'll need is in there. Once you're in the bathroom, if you leave your clothes outside the door, I'll put them in the dryer for you."

"This is beyond the call of duty. You know that, right?"

"I don't think so. You've made me see that some of my past behaviors really did fall short." Those brown eyes held hers until she pulled her gaze away, questioning the depth of what he was saying.

"We were too young to know what we were doing."

After pulling a pair of athletic shorts from a hanger, Sierra entered the bathroom through a wood door that looked original to the cabin. It had a brass doorknob that rattled when she closed the door. Once she'd stripped, she cracked the door open and dropped her clothes on the floor before stepping back inside.

Well, the most she could do was make quick work of her shower. She rallied her last drop of energy to get moving. She gasped that the phenomenal shower behind the frosted door was as large as her entire bathroom at home. It begged her to stay for a while.

After leaving her hearing aids on the vanity, she turned on the faucet. The luxurious space boasted numerous shower heads with various spray-nozzle options. She chose a pulsating one that had an immediate impact on relaxing her muscles.

Wyatt picked up Sierra's clothes from the hall floor. It was ironic that he'd left her one of his office shirts that was worse for wear, given she'd written about his clothes. He tended to appreciate his wardrobe, after everything he'd been through.

He wasn't going to let Sierra, or anyone, make him feel self-conscious about his clothes choices. She hadn't been through what he had. No doubt her father had his faults and after her mother died, she complained about some things, but Joseph Delaney never would have driven his daughter from home by being so critical and impossible to get along with. Everyone thought they knew his history but he hadn't shared the details. After he had run away that awful night of their junior prom, obviously, word had gotten out. The police were involved. But most people didn't know the rest of the story, his story.

He didn't mind surprises. He just didn't like for them to be due to weather. He sure hadn't missed the tornado watches. But in D.C., in the early years he'd lived in some places where police helicopters had shown their lights down on the neighborhood at all hours, in search of criminals. Life had been all about tradeoffs, for him anyway.

With such a negative relationship in his past, he had some serious catching up to do in that department. He would be naïve to think that the problems were all the fault of his ex. Bethany came from troubled past and a less privileged background than his. He'd had a good start in life and that had stayed with him, even though he'd derailed things in his youth.

Being with Sierra, just for these short spurts of time, reminded him of his early days. She brought out the best of his memories. He had more than himself to think about now, though. Max was his concern, so he really couldn't make another mistake with women.

Help me to do what's right, Lord.

Taking the clothes to the dryer and putting out the dog food gave him something productive, to get out of his head. He made his way to the kitchen, refreshed the water bowl and had just poured the food when the sound of running water stopped.

"Eek!" A distressed shriek interrupted his thoughts. He hurried down the hallway while Sadie tore around the corner faster than he'd ever seen her run. Before he reached the bathroom, Sierra burst out of it and rushed toward him, wearing the dress shirt he'd given her. With her hair wet and loose.

Sierra tamped down her terror as she ran down the hall. What was Wyatt's dog doing to her hearing aids? Sadie somehow rattled the old doorknob until she'd gotten into the bathroom and grabbed the hearing aids in her mouth.

"Whoa. No running in the house. Didn't everybody's mom tell them that?" He held out his arm and she stopped, nearly collapsing on his arm, which felt nice and odd at the same time. The little dog had shot out of sight and any damage was probably already done when she grabbed them in the first place.

"And your dog interfering while I'm in the shower was within the rules?"

The idea of him finding out about her secret issue made her stomach clench.

The conversation stalled and Wyatt filled in the gap. "Why'd you let her in there?"

She fumed, envisioning steam spurting out her ears which were empty of what they desperately needed. "I *didn't* let her in."

His eyes widened. "Oh, I see." He winced as the explanation dawned on him. "It's the original door and the fit isn't great. On my long list of repairs. She's only jimmied the doorknob open once before when she smelled treats in my pockets. I'm sorry. What did she do?"

Keep it together, Sierra.

Sierra managed not to wail. "I've got to catch her!" No sooner were the words out than Wyatt's phone rang. She inhaled. At least he would be distracted while she determined how her non-designer hearing wear had survived. Her feet sped along the floors as she turned the corner to the kitchen. Maybe the dog would have lost interest and dropped the hearing aids. She was due for some luck.

Theirs was a dislike-hate relationship but if those four-thousand-dollar gadgets were damaged, she didn't know what she would do. She hadn't even finished paying for them.

Chapter 17

Sadie stood at her dish near the far end of the kitchen, her face buried in the food. A knot of dread formed as big as a bowling ball in Sierra's stomach. Coming closer, she identified the familiar gadgets piled beside the bowl where they'd been tossed for something tastier. She swallowed the lump in her throat and eased her hand out to check that Sadie wouldn't be threatened by a movement toward the food bowl. That was Dog 101 when her mom got their first dog.

Slurps and even a slight growl showed the dog's focus on her meaty chunks was all-consuming. Sierra scooped up the small pieces and let out a breath. The doors of each one held the batteries as they should. She exhaled a breath she hadn't known she was holding. The batteries had not ended up in Sadie's tummy.

Wrung-out as she was, she didn't wish the dog any harm. A

once-over glance of the devices showed that one of the molded earpieces was cracked and gaping open. The other one's tiny wires, that normally stayed compressed tightly together way down inside, were poking out, like a little uncoiled Slinky spring.

The throbbing in her head increased. A boulder lodged in the pit of her stomach. She started to tuck the broken devices into the front pocket of Wyatt's shirt and stopped. He would be sure to see them.

With a quick glance around the huge kitchen, she opted for the windowsill over the sink, hidden behind a blue and white checked cafe curtain. She had barely smoothed the curtain when Wyatt stepped into the far corner of the room. Tears stung the back of her eyes and she swallowed the lump in her throat.

Not only did she have a business on shaky ground, but now she would struggle to hear customers, and everybody else. How long would they take to be fixed and what would it cost? Her audiologist at the university medical center's schedule was always packed and needing repairs hadn't crossed her mind when she bought them.

Wyatt walked in, tucking his phone into his pocket, and came over next to her. "You look like you just lost your biggest customer." At close range, in the silence of the kitchen with him facing her, she figured out what he said without her hearing aids.

All she could do was stare at him, speechless, deciding what to say, what not to say. Her shoulders drooped and she couldn't imagine lifting the weight of them up to where they belonged. If only she could go back in time to when things had been simple, or at least simpler.

He touched her hand and a jolt of electricity shot up her arm. "Tell me…" he said, so low she could barely hear. Exposing her secret would make things easier, in some ways. She would stop thinking about him as anything but a business acquaintance, because he wouldn't want to be with someone who was so conflicted about such a basic part of her life.

They had no future so what difference did it make? She jutted her chin up and was gathering her strength, when Sadie nuzzled her, as though letting her know she was sorry. Frustration bubbled up within her at the dog's big brown eyes looking up at her. Sadie hadn't meant any harm and Sierra appreciated the comforting contact, while she fought the urge to strangle her at the same time. The rubbing continued, methodically, like a soothing balm, and something broke inside Sierra at the comforting gesture.

Wyatt's fingers, softer than she imagined possible, chucked her chin up toward him and he looked into her face. She searched his intense brown eyes. When he put his arm around her, she snuggled in. His muscular frame proved to be the comfort she needed. A look of concern crossed his face. He enveloped her in a closer hug.

Wyatt's muscled body made her aware of how long it'd been since she had been hugged. It was like going home, she wanted to curl up and stay. Could he feel her heart beating fast in her chest? She could get used to this.

From the recesses of her mind, the reasons this was a poor idea came to the surface. She'd been keeping to herself to avoid being uncomfortable about the adjustments the hearing aids called for. So now alarm bells went off in her head, putting her in flight mode. He would discover her secret if she didn't end this wonderful sensation of being in his arms. Maybe just a few seconds longer would be okay. She tried to start pulling back, then remembered.

There's nothing in your ears.

His hand rested on her shoulder. She froze, not wanting to encourage him and unable to break away either. Sooner or later, he would likely know about her hearing aids. But she wanted this moment first, whatever it was.

She looked into his brown eyes, a depth of emotion showing that she hadn't seen before. Attraction and need, maybe gratefulness. Closing the distance between them, he placed his lips on hers, sweet and firm as they melded together.

The kiss ignited something in her and pushed aside any doubts as she leaned in. Putting what he had come to mean to her into the kiss generated a surprising intensity. Finally, she drew back and looked for some message in his eyes, but his gaze only held an invitation for more. They kissed again, and the delicious sensations went right down to her toes.

Chapter 18

Wyatt stood in his kitchen kissing Sierra, her lips soft yet demanding, and only wanting more. A loud clap of thunder cleared his head. He pulled away from her, regretfully. But he needed to focus on the bigger picture, on the circumstances.

Was he making a mistake by kissing her? She had been upset and wouldn't tell him why. The last thing he wanted to do was to take advantage of her when she was vulnerable.

There was no doubt in his mind that she had kissed him back, for sure. With supreme effort, he leaned away and searched Sierra's face for any indecision, signs of regret or hesitation, and found none. He took a step back, their eyes remaining locked in a special intimacy.

He knew with everything in him that he had wanted this

moment, as much as he had tried to hold it back. Maybe fighting what now seemed inevitable had been a mistake. Hopefully, this would get her out of his system and they could get down to the business project and stay there.

Yeah, right.

She was standing in place, seeming to take in the situation, too. Why was their attraction so compelling? Maybe because they had been friends when they were young?

Sadie whined somewhere near his feet. It was her "I-need-to-go-out-now" sound and he knew from experience that she could only wait so long. He gave Sierra a questioning look and her lips turned up at the corners.

"Go on."

Sierra heard the screen door shut with a loud smack as Wyatt went outside with Sadie. She wanted to stand and wait, to savor the kiss. It seemed silly that something so simple had made her feel so deeply.

But she had to move, not think about what would come next. Wyatt would be back any minute. She wanted her own clothes with a fierceness she couldn't explain. On wobbly legs she made it over to the dryer, grabbed her warm clothes with suddenly chilled fingers, and headed to the guest bedroom. Once changed, she hurried back to the sink, and picked up the lightweight gadgets from the windowsill.

Wyatt massaged the back of her neck for a moment and Sierra nearly jumped out of her skin. She hadn't heard him come in. "She took her own sweet time," he said.

Cradling one device in the palm of each hand, she loosely closed her fists and crossed her arms in front of her chest. "I thought Sadie was quick, actually."

I need more time, lots more.

He unsnapped Sadie's leash and she scurried away.

Then he came up beside Sierra and his brown eyes were as black as the night. His scent was fresh from the outdoors, with a tinge of smokiness.

He reached over and touched her arm. He quirked an eyebrow. "What do you have?"

She shrugged. She couldn't find the right words. He had an aw, shucks look on his face. Their kiss had recalibrated their interactions.

He smiled. "Is this still game night? Should we do eeny, meeny, miny, moe?"

Her secret was getting too hard to keep. Unless she wanted an even bigger deal than she ever intended, this game-style reveal worked for her. She'd never thought from the beginning that they'd spend this much time together. Their conversation tonight had convinced her she would be fine, in any case. She didn't know why she had ever thought otherwise.

She unfolded her arms and held out her fists. He chanted the words from their childhood and when he landed on her right fist, she turned over her hand and went ahead and opened both fists.

One dark eyebrow hitched up. "Where'd those come from?"

Sierra swallowed. Omitting information was one thing. But flat-out lying was something else altogether. "They're m-m-mine." Great. She hadn't realized her voice would come out high pitched like that.

The crease in his forehead deepened, as he studied her. "Since when?" His words were slow and deliberate. She heard him perfectly, at least. They were in an ideal set-up for someone with bum ears. The room was quiet, and Wyatt stood near enough that she got clues from a little lip reading.

"A few weeks." She gave a stiff shrug hoping he would buy her fake nonchalance.

"Seems I remember you had to be retested when they checked hearing in school."

She nodded, surprised that he'd remember such a detail about her. There was no denying their history went deep.

But they couldn't escape how clunky the hearing aids were. What she could do was act like she didn't care and it was no big deal.

He studied the hearing aids and his smile faded. "They look like they're in bad shape." She choked back the sob that clogged her throat. Something about him knowing how mangled they were made the discussion more real.

He frowned and his next words came out slower. "This is why you were chasing Sadie?" Maybe it was her imagination but he seemed to be talking a lot slower. "She did this." Again, he dragged out the words. Annoyance bubbled up. People seemed to automatically exaggerate their words when they found out she couldn't hear.

"Wow, great observation."

The hurt in his eyes came and went so quickly she almost missed it. "This is my fault and I'm going to fix them or get you new ones. Now, why didn't you tell me?"

She blinked the tears that pricked behind her eyes. She wouldn't cry. She pointed her chin a little bit higher toward him.

"It's personal? I didn't want you to treat me differently."

His shoulders sagged.

"Whatever you thought of me all these years, you must know I wouldn't hurt you, or ever treat you differently."

"Yes, you will. Everybody does. They don't mean to…" *Stop making excuses for other people.* She had to get away or the dam would break.

"I won't. I promise. I hope you can forgive me for an honest question. How are you hearing me now, without them?"

"When I'm in a quiet room and we're this close, through a combination of lip reading and paying really close attention, I can have a conversation." She smiled, "Listening to a nice, deep voice like yours helps too."

There was no point in arguing. In saying how people talked differently to people with hearing loss. How strangers thought your brain was smaller because of the hearing aids.

"It doesn't matter to me," he said.

"Maybe it does to me." She walked away from him. "Do you

have something I can put these in?"

Wyatt went to a cabinet and opened the door to pull out a plastic container. "Here you go."

She put them in it and made sure the lid was sealed. "Thanks. This is something I'm obviously going to have to adjust to. Now that I've faced that my hearing loss requires hearing aids, I still might have to have conversations explaining how to help me. I'm just not quite there yet. But I will be. They don't fix everything, like wearing glasses can bring your vision to 20/20, but I hear better than before, so that's good."

"Look, I get it. I'm really sorry. I'll get them repaired and things'll be better."

"You always liked rescuing. I'm a big girl now and can handle this myself."

Sierra wasn't at all sure that she could cope well with it. If one hour with one dead battery had been such a disaster, how awful would it be to wait days or weeks to get these fixed, or for new ones to come in if that's what it took? Now that her secret was out, she actually felt a little better, relieved even.

"You never did like accepting help, and you wouldn't be needing it now if I had fixed that door, or paid closer attention to my dog. I'm responsible for the situation you're in and I'm going to make it right."

He said, "First thing in the morning, I'd really like to take you to the doctor and get this straightened out."

"What? I am certainly capable of driving myself."

"Of course. I didn't mean to imply otherwise. But will you

please let me go? It'll be easier for me to help and to pay. We don't know what this is going to take." He looked at Sadie curled up in her dog bed, then up at a clock on the wall.

Wyatt might need a reality check. "I'm afraid it isn't that simple. They book weeks in advance for regular appointments, is all I know."

"There's always a way." He gave her a look she couldn't interpret, then pulled something out of a cabinet. "Don't tell anyone about this. You'll wreck my macho image, but I do this to unwind." Pulling his hand away so she could see what he'd put on the counter, he proceeded to remove a wrapped teabag from a box. "Care to join me? We'll figure everything out. Those tornadoes worry me. I actually texted Caleb, a construction titan, while you were showering and he said that your place definitely wasn't sturdy. My guest bedroom is the better choice."

It'd been a long day and she didn't want Wyatt to be alone tonight, so maybe this was meant to be. "I'd like to. I mean, I'd like tea and your guest room sounds great."

There was comfort in the company of others. Who was she kidding? She didn't want to get bogged down in the "What ifs" or "What will this lead to?" when thinking about Wyatt. She wanted to stay and she would. It was as simple as that.

While he fixed the tea, lightning strikes continued outside, making light flashes in the windows and the occasional loud boom of thunder.

He brought her a cup of tea and they sat together at his little table, so close she could hear his deep voice just fine. She cupped her hands around her drink, letting the warmth seep in. "I like when nature takes control," she said.

"I think of it more as God expressing himself through nature. But it never hurts to be reminded of who's in charge."

They sipped on their tea until their cups were empty.

Wyatt stood and carried their things to the sink. "My brother Gage slept in the guest room last and the housekeeper hasn't been here. I need to put clean sheets on."

Sierra watched Wyatt make preparations for the guest bedroom and felt bad for inconveniencing him. But his dog had caused so much trouble, so maybe they weren't close to being even.

After he busied himself by getting sheets and they put them on together, he tucked the comforter on top and tossed her a pillow to help with a pillowcase. Without thinking, she tossed it right back.

Wyatt caught the pillow. "There you go, get rid of some of that pent-up frustration." From the way his chest and his mouth were, she knew he was talking louder than he normally would. He pelted the pillow back at her.

She touched it for a second and zipped it back at his head. "Frustrated doesn't begin to cover it."

But throwing the pillow lightened her mood. Suddenly, she couldn't help but smile at how ridiculous this was. She had been self-conscious about the hearing aids, and now she couldn't use them and she was going to miss how they helped her. She couldn't have it both ways. She needed to come to some peace about it.

She wasn't a wimp and didn't put up with being treated badly, but she didn't like to hold a grudge either. Partly, she'd always had trouble staying mad at Wyatt for very long. She was all about making the best of things and making up when feelings had been hurt. Her next throw aimed the pillow right for his face.

He blocked the blow with one arm. "Anyone ever told you about passive aggressive tendencies?" He located the pillow and placed it on the bed.

She grabbed a vase in the shape of a cowboy boot from the dresser and took aim. "Don't believe so. Straight-out aggressive, yes."

"There's a first time for everything."

She set the vase back where it belonged. Their first kiss was what lingered in her mind. It was too bad that was a one-time thing.

"You're right, what you said, I don't like needing help." Wyatt turned and studied her. "I've not been handling my hearing loss well and now without hearing aids it's going to be even worse."

"I'm—"

She interrupted him and he leaned against the door jam, listening to her. "Thank you for the way you've handled this, for listening to me rant, and for trying to understand how I feel."

He came over and wrapped her in a quick hug. Pulling the door shut behind him on his way out, he said, "Sleep well." She leaned on the closed door for a while after he'd gone. It had been quite a night.

Sierra found some PJ's in the dresser that fit her close

enough, pretty sure she wouldn't be getting much sleep tonight. She brushed her teeth and flashed a smile at her reflection in the mirror. Clearing the air about their past and sharing the truth about her hearing with Wyatt seemed to have taken a weight off her shoulders. She suddenly felt lighter in both body and spirit.

With the way things were going, who knew what tomorrow would bring?

She wasn't at all sure if she wanted to find out.

Chapter 19

Wyatt looked out the kitchen window at Galloway Farm, shot up a quick prayer for God's blessing on his day, and enjoyed the visual feasts of the crops growing in the fields. Soybeans were prettier than any architecture he'd ever seen, he decided. The scent of his coffee wafted up, waking him as much as the sip of "full-bodied liquid," according to the label. He'd called over to Caleb's first-thing and Max was doing well.

Another kiss from Sierra would be perfect.

He must be losing his fool mind. Getting the solar panels running on the farm and being a good dad to Max, those were enough on his plate. And now he had to get Sierra's hearing aids fixed.

Yet all he wanted to do was stare at Galloway Sons' beautiful soybeans and fantasize about kisses.

Last night he couldn't have been more surprised that Sierra wore hearing aids. She obviously had some issues with it, in spite of her jokes. She had no idea how beautiful she was, and how hard it was for him to see her wrestle with something that had no impact on how he felt about her. The struggles were a result of her high standard of expectation for everything, he was sure. At such a vulnerable time, when she was clearly upset about something, maybe he shouldn't have kissed her.

Not that he regretted the moment. Not at all.

Seeing her struggling with something, even when he didn't know what it was, had touched him. She had always had exceptional self-confidence. Her life had been far from perfect but she always stood on her own two feet and had never needed him for anything.

"Good morning." Sierra stood at the entrance to the kitchen, her hair loose around her shoulders. Her hazel-green eyes brought even more light into the huge, sun-filled room. "May I join you?"

She moved into the room swiftly, partly to hear better, he presumed. He made sure to speak clearly, at a normal speed, and close to his usual volume. "Are you a coffee drinker?"

She smiled and spoke softly, like she was still waking up. "No, but I've always loved the scent so carry on."

He was having trouble concentrating on the conversation. "Didn't think so. I took up the habit later."

She stretched her arms up high and then rolled out her

shoulders, one at a time. "There's nothing like waking up on a farm. I used to love waking up at Granny's."

He turned to the cabinet, pawing through the glasses looking for a favorite mug. "I'm going to put the rest of this in a to-go mug. Care to come along to make the rounds to check on the animals?"

He turned around, filled up the glass in his hand. Sierra was still standing where she had been, a pained look on her face. She walked over close to him. "I can't tell what you're saying when you talk with your back to me like that."

He frowned. There was so much he didn't understand, so many mistakes waiting for him to make. "I'm sorry. I didn't know."

She bit her lip, and when she spoke, her voice had a slight shake. "It isn't your fault. The thing is, I want to venture out socially more than I have in the past few years. That will involve my teaching people how to help me to hear them better. And I hate that. Not sure I'm up for it."

He touched her hand, which lit a spark of heat that felt so right he wanted to leave it there. But he didn't and pulled away. "Anyone who cares will be willing to learn. I know I am." He smiled and looked directly into her beautiful green eyes, moving his lips distinctly and speaking clearly. "My to-go cup is ready. Would you like to take a walk?"

"Lead the way."

He grabbed a chilled bottle of water from the fridge as they left, handing it to her outside.

"You remembered."

"You'd be surprised how much." The skin around her eyes crinkled when she smiled. Just one of the little things he hoped to find out about as they got to know each other.

The ground was wet under foot from the rain but the sun already beat down as they entered the barn.

A large, majestic black horse poked its head over the gate. Wyatt patted the horse's neck and leaned close to Sierra, speaking directly to her. "Remember Lucinda?"

"How could I forget? She ran away with me once."

Her nearness was intoxicating, and spending time together meant he could enjoy things about her that he hadn't noticed before. She wore a heart bracelet on her wrist and earrings that continued the heart theme sparkled when she turned her head.

He stood nearer yet. "She mellowed over the years. By the way, I like having an excuse to stand closer to you." She blushed as he went on to explain. "Well, this is her granddaughter. Meet Louise."

He reached into his pocket for a sugar cube he offered to the beautiful animal. The horse's gentle mouth on his hand still intrigued him as much as when he was young. Its whiskers tickled. He'd already introduced Max to Louise, aware of the generations. His dad had shown him horses.

"You used to let me ride whenever I wanted to," Sierra said. "Once you left, I realized I'd taken it all for granted."

"You weren't the only one. There were so many times I wanted to come back. My pride, mainly, wouldn't let me. When

I started finding some success and got an internship that opened the door to my future, I thought I was fine. That it was okay no one I met had anything in common with my upbringing. Morals, even. Faith."

Not the way you and I do, after spending just days together.

He needed to slow down these thoughts that wanted to race ahead. *Just enjoy the moment.* She was near enough for him to see the flecks in her eyes. Sunlight shone in the window above the haymow, and sparks of dust from the straw danced in the sunbeams.

They would be good together.

But he'd been down this road before. One thing he knew. He wasn't husband material. Married life was not for him.

Was it? He needed to tell his racing heart that. And why was he even thinking about the M Word? Because she had him feeling what he'd never felt before and believing in more than had ever been.

He motioned her out of the barn to take a walk next to the fence line. They strolled along, each alone with their thoughts.

All he knew was Bethany and his relationship was toxic. Not having any relationships to observe up close once he moved out, he wasn't sure how all that was supposed to work.

Could he be there for another person the way devoted couples were? What would it be like to plan with someone well matched, to go through life with someone who shared your interests?

In quiet companionship, they looked out at the Black Angus cattle, then headed back to the house. The storm damage had been minimal. Strong winds could be selective, taking down a barn and touching nothing for miles. They'd been lucky, from some news reports he'd heard. He'd need to put someone on cleaning up the limbs on the ground, though. The water trough had overflowed with rain but things were basically in good shape.

"I can't wait any longer. I've got to go see Max at the main house. Miss my buddy."

"Of course." His stride was much longer than hers but he noted she kept up with almost two steps to his one.

Sierra spoke, her voice breathy from keeping up with him. "He's a cutie. It's obvious he's had the best of care."

"You know how to warm a dad's heart. Once he's in a routine, he'll sleep better. Don't hold anything I've said against me. I'm chronically sleep deprived." If only he could blame going in to kiss her on lack of sleep, he would. "The college students I have caring for him all take different shifts and now Aunt Elizabeth is on board, which should help."

"I know you're trying for a nanny, but that could be a while. The thing is, by giving him several rotating sitters from the college, he never settles into a routine. And he's a social butterfly, interacts with each person who cares for him, which can over stimulate him."

This. This was why he needed to proceed with caution in a relationship. What she'd said might be true but her words came across as judgmental. Or maybe he was just sensitive where Max was concerned? But he really didn't want anyone weighing in on what he did.

"Where'd you get your experience with kids?" He sounded grouchy to his own ears.

"Have you forgotten? When we were younger, I was the neighborhood babysitter."

He didn't know how to respond, feeling a grumpiness he couldn't explain. "Well, my kid's more special than those kids you're remembering."

She reached up on tiptoe and her lips brushed his. Her touch drove everything from his mind and he leaned into their kiss until she pulled away. "Max sure is a lucky little boy to have you for a dad," she said, sounding slightly out of breath. She linked her arm in his and they walked on until they reached their destination.

As soon as they stepped into the main house, little Max spotted his daddy and let out a squeal. A lump formed in Wyatt's throat. Was there anything better than this? He waved at his boy, went in for a quick hug so he didn't disturb his eating. Without hesitation, Sierra leaned down and gave Max a kiss, more like a peck, on his cheek. He giggled and gave her the biggest grin.

Wyatt's doubts receded somewhat. Maybe with the right person, someone as caring as Sierra, they could make it work together? He pointed Sierra toward a couple of empty chairs at the farm kitchen's long table and followed her where they took seats.

"Woot!" Caleb's girlfriend, Annie, shot up from her chair at the end of the table. "You go, girl!" She'd shouted so loud, it appeared Sierra heard her, since her face flushed pink. Annie came to her and turned her around. "Just the person I needed to see. Let's have a quick meeting in the home office."

The two women sauntered off, arms around one another's shoulders.

Upon closer inspection, Wyatt sent up a prayer they wouldn't be gone long, since the children around here outnumbered the men now.

Chapter 20

Sierra followed Annie into a room she'd never seen before. Annie closed the door behind them and gave Sierra a hug. "What're you doing here?"

Fortunately, Annie talked louder when she was excited, and she was practically shrieking directly in Sierra's face. She could hear just fine. Sierra decided on the direct approach. "It isn't what you may think."

Annie's face fell. "Oh, I maybe had unrealistic expectations."

Sierra laughed out loud, tempted to roll on the floor for good measure. "I mean, what did you think? Well, maybe I don't want to know, so let me recap. You knew that Wyatt stayed after the concessions closed at the game last night, since you guys were celebrating with Chloe. We ended up having the longest, deepest, heart-to-heart conversation." She paced around the room. "And then the storm was coming, I stayed at his house last night, and his dog tried to eat my hearing aids."

Annie's mouth had dropped open and stayed there. "So why are you so happy?"

"I'm not sure that I am. I'm probably in shock or hysterical to be honest. I mean, my hearing aids are a mess. Now Wyatt knows I wear hearing aids, which I really didn't want, just dealing with them is annoying. But here's the thing. He told me more about what happened after he left. It's like a huge mystery has been solved. That's all I know. That's pretty much all I've got."

"How'd he react to the news about your hearing aids?"

Sierra sat down on a big leather sofa, the kind only a woman would buy that only a man would be comfortable sitting in. "Wonderfully. Honestly, he's said the nicest things to me."

"I knew he would be one of the good guys, Sierra. I think we all make assumptions about people, both positive and negative. And the Galloways look like they have everything, in terms of possessions, but their character is what really makes them stand out, once you get to know them."

The sofa seemed to swallow her up like brown-leather quicksand. Spreading her arms around herself, she gave a great big hug. After talking with Wyatt so intensely last night, having her hearing aids damaged, and their "first kiss," she needed all the self-care she could manage.

Annie's mouth appeared to be permanently open. "There are so many details I'm missing here! But we've got to get back in there. The kids will tear those men up limb from limb if we don't.'

Sierra waved a hand. "Oh, they can hold the fort down for another minute."

"Maybe you're right. So do you like Wyatt? You know, *like* like him?"

Sierra stood up. "This is why we're meeting? I thought you wanted direction for running Delaney's while I'm going to be gone this afternoon."

"Are you kidding me? Well, I can imagine this is a bit overwhelming and I know what I'd do."

She did feel a bit overloaded with stimulation but would figure it out herself. "About what?"

Annie smacked her hand onto her forehead, "About Wyatt, silly!"

"I don't even know." She paused. "He's great at kissing though."

Annie hugged her and they confirmed their schedules for the next couple of days. Then they went back to the big dining room where the kids were with the men.

Wyatt sat at the kitchen table that had been the site of many family dinners. He hadn't even known how much he'd loved mealtime and other Galloway traditions until after he was gone. At their own table with their highchairs pulled up to it, Ella and Drew looked more like twins than he'd ever seen them look before, in PJ's that matched the ones Max was also wearing.

With the same dark hair, and brown eyes, and perfect little

noses, all three babies looked like siblings. At the table, nearest to them, Annie had returned from some kind of secret meeting with Sierra. Annie resumed doling out the small, round-oat cereals. Little fingers scooped them up and smashed them into their mouths as fast as she supplied them.

Chloe sat next to her mother and ate cereal and milk from a bowl. She held up a cornflake "Can you say 'one,' Drew?"

The little boy studied her and Chloe repeated the word, slowly. "One."

Finally, after Wyatt had given up hope, Drew said, "Buh!"

Chloe clapped. "Mommy, he was so close!" Annie smiled.

Caleb stood at the stove with bacon sizzling in a pan. His brother looked genuinely happy, which was perhaps more than he could say for himself. "We wondered how that storm treated you last night since we left early. Just wanted you to know I've set up a wing of this place for Annie and Chloe to stay sometimes. We decided last night was that time. Aunt Elizabeth insisted on going home or we would have put her up in one of the guest rooms."

Wyatt really appreciated having so much living space and all the luxuries his family enjoyed. "That's one of the advantages to having so much land and so many buildings. Sierra and I came to a similar conclusion, decided it'd be best if she spent the night in my guest room."

There was a little shot-out of "woot!" Annie was at it again. It was a side of her that Wyatt hadn't seen. Caleb rolled his eyes at her. Wyatt wasn't sure they had known one another long enough to be talking marriage. After his experience, he wanted to put the brakes on rushing into anything and thought everyone else should too.

He glanced at Sierra sitting next to him. Something about last night had brought out the defender in him. Sticking close had been the only way he could think of to help her, to be her ears for her. An added bonus was having an excuse to spend more time with her. But it was way more than her hearing challenges, due to his dog, that had him evaluating everything. She'd helped him plumb the depths of his soul somehow. Which sounded ridiculous except he had been there, and he believed what he was saying. He crossed the room, leaned down, and hugged his son again.

"I'm covering for Sierra at the diner all day today," Annie said. "Chloe's going to be Caleb's helper with these two."

Wyatt needed to get used to sharing his plans, too. He'd become more shut off than he'd realized. "Chloe, do you think you could tend to Max, too, with Caleb's help?"

The little girl bobbed her head up and down. "I sure can. We're going to play school and I need more students."

Given how teaching Drew to say "one" had worked out, he wasn't so sure. "That sounds fine." He looked at the others. "Turns out Sierra and I are going to make a run to Indy, to check on—"

Sierra interrupted. "Adapting a wardrobe for Wyatt that fits his Galloway Farm of Fair Creek life better."

Wyatt blinked. But okay, so they weren't going to say anything about repairing the hearing aids then. Maybe change took time and he would give Sierra whatever space she needed. Caleb looked up from plating the bacon and gave Wyatt a pointed look, like he needed backed up on what she'd said. The man knew him too well. He did not go shopping without a fight.

Wyatt nodded. "Bringing all my city clothes here was only going to work for so long."

Annie chimed in, giving a thumbs up. "I approve."

Caleb waved the spatula in her direction. "Now, no ganging up on Wyatt, Honey. He'll have to see something he likes before he commits. Shopping breaks us Galloway sons out in hives, so you've been warned. We prefer to live in the luxury we have earned for ourselves and use personal shoppers, when necessary. For Vortex Clean Energy's Initial Public Offering, he worked with one from New York City, to make his debut on the floor of the New York Stock Exchange."

The women shared wide-eyed looks. "I would like to have seen the clothing chosen," Sierra said. "What can I say? Fashion intrigues me!"

They all dug into their breakfast, enjoying their meal and stretching their time together. The waffles and syrup, fresh-squeezed orange juice, and hash browns were the best he'd tasted since he couldn't remember when. The cinnamon roll from Fair Creek's own Sweet Shop bakery was worth the sugar coma he felt coming on. He didn't know if baked goods made locally the same morning just tasted that much better or if the food was extra tasty from seeing the smiling faces surrounding him and having Sierra by his side.

Finally, he felt like he'd explode if he took one more bite so he stood to carry his plate to the sink.

Caleb scrambled up from the big wood chair at the head of the table and stood. "Hold up a minute. Might as well tell you all together."

Everyone looked his way, and even the babies stopped smacking spoons on their highchair trays.

"I went to the lawyer yesterday and I've been processing things ever since." Wyatt sat back down to give his full attention as Caleb went on. "These kids' mom continues to fight her addiction. Our sister does." He picked up his water glass and took a long swallow. "She's making some headway, not what we'd hoped. But things have deteriorated with the dad. They're not sure where he is."

No one said anything. Kayla's troubles were just one more reason Wyatt regretted being out of the picture. He probably couldn't have helped her if he'd stayed, but you never knew. He wished he'd tried.

"So, I've thought it over and I don't want to push for termination of parental rights. Drew and Ella are fine here with me. With us." He looked around the room. Annie dabbed the corner of her eye with a napkin. "I've prayed about it. We're going to leave the door open for Kayla to pull herself together. I don't want to remove the possibility of her having her kids one day, which might give her an incentive to keep fighting whatever she's going through."

Caleb looked at Drew and Ella. "I have to be able to live with whatever story I tell these guys when they're older. They need to know I tried everything for them to be with their mom, as much as I can't imagine parting with them."

Annie blew her nose with a honking sound.

Caleb picked up the glass again and took a swallow. He cleared his throat and swiped his hand across his face.

Wyatt walked over and shook his brother's hand and patted him on the shoulder. "I'll be here for you. It might be easier, in some ways, to close that door as you put it. But sometimes the easy way isn't what's best. Maybe it never is."

If he'd stayed and worked things out with Dad, how would things have been different? What if he had been the connection Kayla needed?

The babies began making a racket with their spoons, interrupting his thoughts. No point in dwelling on the past. He was here now, and it felt more right than anything had in a while. That was what mattered.

If he could just get through the day with Sierra. Could the hearing aids be repaired? And this shopping trip she'd planned and sprung on him seemed doomed from the start. He hadn't shopped for himself in years. Other people brought things to him.

Maybe he was worrying too much. What could possibly go wrong?

Chapter 21

Wyatt stood on his front porch and enjoyed Sierra's dancing green eyes as she approached him. "Are you ready?" Her cheerful attitude gave him hope. She'd run home to change clothes and "throw on" some make-up, as she called it, for their trip to Indy. Her gold neon T-shirt and dark jeans with high-topped sneakers in complementary colors conveyed a festive mood.

"I'd be lying if I didn't admit I'm concerned about what you've got planned." Her reddish curly hair flowed down around her shoulders. Now he knew why she had adapted that style she had for work. His heart rate kicked up a notch. He had to accept that she would always have that effect on him. Maybe he needed to get used to it. A man didn't have to act on everything he felt.

Her eyes sparkled and she grinned. "You have to trust me."

"Have I mentioned I have trust issues?"

She was so fun to be around. Her hearing aids really didn't make any difference to him, and telling her that now might bring the topic all back for her. She probably wouldn't believe him anyway, because the aids clearly had flipped her thinking about herself somehow.

"Well, this little exercise will be perfect because, um, well, face the fear and all that."

He wanted so much to be there for her and possibly make up for his mistakes in the past, the times he had thought more of himself than of her. Last night had made him see that he really could have done better.

She tugged his sleeve. Whoops. Had he been staring at her?

"Come on, you were right, and I've figured out a way to have these babies looked at today." She held up a small, sturdy plastic case the hearing aids must have come in. It had a logo he was unfamiliar with that was probably created by the medical company that had developed them.

"How I wish they were in their container last night, but it was all spur-of-the-moment. Hey, what's gotten into you? You're at a higher energy level." Maybe his being there for her was already helping. He couldn't imagine that was true. But if he could help her in some way, he would.

Sierra shrugged. "Beats me."

Well, if she refused to talk about last night, he wasn't going to bring it up. He'd been completely surprised about her revelation. And a little hurt that she hadn't trusted him. Certainly not repulsed as she seemed to think. He appreciated her vulnerability and respected her all the more.

"Maybe being on the farm is having a positive impact on me. City living really can be kind of a rat race. The traffic especially. This is more peaceful. I'm enjoying it more than I anticipated."

He led her out to Caleb's truck that he'd loaned them since he was sticking close to home today. She hopped up onto the seat and he couldn't help but notice how her jeans accentuated her ample curves.

He had to tamp down these feelings of attraction if they were going to spend time together. But he took it as a good sign that he was responding to her, since he hadn't found any woman that interested him since Bethany passed.

He wasn't going to do anything about it. Just stick to business. Maybe if the right opportunity arose, he'd think of something to help her mindset about the hearing aids, though. *Give me the words, Lord.*

He might as well play along with her plans. "What's on our agenda?"

"First stop, heading to the doctor's. Then we'll go clothes shopping to bring your wardrobe in line with Fair Creek standards." She grinned.

"I can only hope to rise to that level. Shopping with you will be a whole new experience, I have no doubt." Tension built up in his chest remembering Bethany, who he had allowed to arrange his every move when he first left home. This trip of Sierra's wasn't about interfering with his independence, was it? His ability to gauge relationships was just so skewed.

"Keep an open mind, is all I ask, and you'll find something you like, I feel confident."

"Whatever you say, Chief. Anything after that?"

"It's a surprise."

Maybe he'd be able to relax, given how much he enjoyed spending time with her. There was too much at stake to go into any dating situation lightly.

Was he thinking about dating?

"Should I be worried you'll make me into a redneck?"

"You? Not a chance. That's beyond even my wardrobing skills."

He tilted his head and gave her a thoughtful look. "If there's a compliment in there somewhere, I'll take it."

One thing was for sure, she would keep him on his toes, just as she always had.

Chapter 22

Sierra enjoyed the light, fun chat she carried on with Wyatt all the way to Indianapolis. That kept her mind off of the reason for their trip. When they hit the city limits, a knot formed in her stomach that grew as the medical facility came into view.

Wyatt parked in an adjacent lot and they were inside in no time. When she'd called earlier, she learned that the doctor's office held clinics once a week for fixed hours to expedite hearing aid repairs for those who needed them. They walked in the office to a sign that read "clinic today."

Sierra signed in. "Sadie's timing was good, anyway. Getting a private appointment would have taken forever."

They sat down to wait and each became engrossed in their phone screens. While some time passed, Sierra noticed children coming in wearing hearing aids. Some of their devices were multi-colored. They were young and didn't appear to be self-conscious.

Their optimism and general high spirits reminded her of the Bible verse about a little child leading them. Maybe God was answering her prayer in an unexpected way. Maybe she'd ended up here to learn acceptance from these kids who faced greater challenges than she did. Her hearing loss had begun as an adult, after her speech had fully developed. She needed to appreciate this blessing.

Finally, her name was called, and she and Wyatt went in, as they had agreed. The technician examined the hearing aids. "What happened?"

"A dog got them," Sierra said.

"Sorry to hear that. This happens more than you might think. They smell a person's scent and are drawn to medical devices like hearing aids and orthodontic retainers. Let me have a look. I'll be back."

He left the room.

Wyatt looked down to where her hands were in her lap, and she realized she had been wringing her hands like her aunt used to do.

Wyatt said, "I can't tell you how sorry I am."

He'd apologized enough. She didn't want him to feel bad. "You couldn't have known this would happen. It is interesting that dogs do this sort of thing regularly, isn't it? Now I'll know to keep them put away when animals are around. If I hadn't been so new to this, it might not have happened."

"Well, this seems like a nightmare for you."

"I don't want to look at it that way. This will be resolved, one way or the other, and then I'll be up and running."

After about ten minutes the technician returned. "I'm afraid I've got bad news. The aids can't be repaired. I'm sorry."

Her shoulders sagged as she let the information sink in. She didn't have any money and still owed on these that were damaged. She couldn't let Wyatt pay for the whole things.

He definitely seemed committed to his plan. "What is the fastest possible method to get a new pair? I'll pay for expediting the order."

The man looked toward Sierra. "I've consulted with the doctor on your behalf. We're a teaching hospital and recently were approved to sell an updated hearing aid. We're recommending you get that." His enthusiasm was contagious.

Sierra wasn't sure. "That sounds expensive."

"To get people to try them, they're priced three percent lower than the pair you have."

Wyatt had a smile on his face. "I'm always for upgrading."

"I couldn't let you pay."

She nodded to the man. "May we discuss this alone for a minute?"

He stepped outside of the room.

Sierra turned to Wyatt. "Realistically, paying you back may not be in the foreseeable future." But she had to believe in herself and needed to think positively about her long-term opportunities.

Giving herself the best possible chance to maximize her hearing played a part in that.

"It really is my place, because of how your current hearing aids were damaged. I can well afford it and you're helping me out with my business, and your services would be quite expensive. So it all works out. I sure won't be knocking on your door to be repaid, if that's what you're worried about."

"There's some logic to what you're saying. I hadn't thought of it that way. I will take you up on it."

Sierra stared out the window on the long ride home. Her new devices wouldn't be in for a week, at least. In the meantime, she'd be stuck saying "huh?" a gazillion times a day. The thought of it exhausted her. She had hoped that, if Wyatt ever found out, she would be in a position of strength, and be fully adjusted to the hearing aids and coping well. Now this. He'd seen her at her most vulnerable. Yet she still felt optimistic. He really was the great person she'd always thought he was.

As they drove away from the doctor's office after they were told the old ones were too damaged to fix, Wyatt could tell Sierra was in a bad mood. He couldn't blame her and felt some responsibility for the way she felt. He tried to think about how he could help. She had a setback but things would be fine as soon as he got the hearing aids replaced.

Maybe conversation would be good to lighten the mood.

"Why are you so committed to your business?"

He suspected that she struggled to hear him, even though he tried to speak up. The only problem? The truck Wyatt had borrowed from Caleb had a huge cab that separated them. The usual road sounds didn't help, either. It felt like he needed to yell.

"Plain and simple, Delaney's is Aunt Lucy's legacy and my mother and grandmother helped some too. That's worth preserving."

"True. I also believe your aunt's legacy is in the hearts of all the people she served, including me and my family. Nothing can take that away."

Her look showed appreciation in her eyes. "I care about my own legacy, too. I want to do something good for this little town that supported me after Mom died and Dad was gone so much."

He quirked an eyebrow. "That's all good but maybe you just like seeing your name in lights, not literally. But as the owner, you are known to your customers. And it got you named as mayor."

"Come on, you know Fair Creek doesn't have a mayor. But I'm absolutely working in the business for the recognition." She laughed. "It's a glamorous life but someone has to do it."

He hoped the conversation was lifting her spirits. "I hate to see anyone's heart and soul tied up in a business endeavor. It's really difficult to run a restaurant and there's a high failure-rate."

At a stoplight, she looked in his direction. "Yeah, the restaurant and my hearing are both things I deal with and would challenge anyone. Sometimes I blame myself for not coping better, when showing acceptance and adapting to the situation would be more constructive than the frustration I sometimes feel."

He faced her. "I can see what you're saying. Hey, I asked because I'm hoping to be working alongside you."

"What do you mean?"

"I'd like to be alongside you, to be your ears, just until your new hearing aids are ready to go."

"I can't ask you to do that."

"You didn't ask. I offered and I insist."

She looked out the window for a few seconds, making him wonder what she thought.

"That is nice of you and I must admit that there's a possibility I might need some assistance. But instead of committing, can we just see how it goes?"

"Yes, of course. That makes sense."

"Great. I appreciate your understanding. And on another note, let's set up the time for me to come learn about you and your business."

"When should I come? We could do it at Delaney's if that helps."

"I'd rather come to your place, if you don't mind. It should be quieter and I'll have fewer distractions. Max could be there, too, so there won't be babysitter issues."

Chapter 23

They arrived at the clothing store and Wyatt felt surprisingly upbeat about shopping. He did what he usually did at a new adventure. Tried to learn what he could from the experience.

"So what exactly are we shopping for?"

"This! We're shopping for this." Sierra had stopped, standing by a display of T-shirts. All of them named the July Fourth weekend in bright lettering, featured the year, included a US flag and the store logo. "I think you all could use these for branding. We could get these for every Galloway, from the littlest ones to the vintage ones. Introduce them on the fourth."

"I love the idea. By the way…" he said. Other than when he thought about Max, he wasn't used to this. He had a full-blown family, and they were going to be in matching T-shirts on a holiday.

Sierra just looked at him as he processed it. "We, meaning the Galloway Sons Farm, as in, my family. We're inviting the town of Fair Creek out to the farm for a picnic after the parade. It's short notice, but I'm assigned to order the food and would love for you to do it. There's so much going on that I forgot. I'm sorry."

"What a fantastic idea. Thank you for thinking of me, of Delaney's."

"Who else would there be? You're our favorite."

Sierra touched her palm to her heart. "How sweet of you to say. I don't take anything for granted, hope I never do. I'm grateful. Can we work on the menu on the way home?"

"Yes, we can."

They had to figure out how many shirts they needed for the Galloway clan and what sizes. When they were done, they set out to shop for clothes for Wyatt.

"You know how I feel about your suits and ties," she said as they walked around the men's section. "Don't get me wrong. You look terrific. It's just that you stand out like a scoop of chocolate nestled in a pint of vanilla ice cream."

"I've done extremely well in business with my current clientele. "

"I'm sure you have and most of your customers dress like you do."

He nodded. "Even if their work didn't require them to dress like me, they appreciated my professional look."

She nodded. "Well, that was D.C. When I worked in advertising, a farmer might come in from the field to talk about his campaign to promote seed sales one day and an attorney running for office wanting to get into politics would come in the next. I learned to put people at ease by dressing similar to them."

"You're suggesting I wear overalls when I talk to farmers?"

"No, that's not what I'm saying. In your situation, you're trying to persuade a community that you can relate to them, that you mean them no harm. Just wear something that looks like you belong here, or at least that you don't belong somewhere else. Like in a city." She grinned. "Blend in with the community and put people at ease."

"Are you sure all this coaching is necessary?"

He came to a stop and she looked over at him. She returned his look and he saw the gold flecks in her green eyes.

"In a word. Yes."

"This is news to me, and I don't quite believe you. Just sayin.'"

"Well, even if it weren't necessary, I wouldn't pass up a chance to boss you around."

He didn't think his heart could beat any faster. He enjoyed their interaction too much to dwell on the fact that he wasn't totally in charge, as he preferred to be. How did he know Sierra was not like women in his past relationships?

She went to a rack and pulled out a pair of boot cut jeans and a collared shirt that would be wrong in an office and perfect in Fair Creek. "Try these." She went to shelves of jeans and grabbed some different styles, then sorted through a rack and selected a teal plaid shirt she said would look great with his coloring.

"The dressing rooms are over there."

When he walked out wearing the pair of jeans he liked best and the teal shirt with his Stetson and his boots, he watched for her reaction.

She blinked once, and then twice, at the sight of him. Her cheeks flushed a slight pink.

"That's a good look on you. But what do *you* think?"

"Oh, now you're going to pretend I have a vote?"

"Don't be ridiculous. Of course, you have a say."

How flustered she became turned out to be all he needed to know. She seemed to respond positively and had made him into a believer. Maybe walking in the shoes of Fair Creek residents made sense.

After some tweaking for size and additional colors, they walked out with a new wardrobe for him. Sierra looked exceptionally pleased with herself, with a wide, satisfied smile on her face while carrying a large bag. Wyatt was more convinced that he didn't want to completely leave his suits behind. With the size of his bank account, dropping some money on clothes didn't mean anything to him. If he changed his mind, he could give these away to a charity. Maybe he would go slowly on changing his clothing choices so he could relax and come to know the people of Fair Creek as his true self.

He needed to get used to dressing down. Anything was worth a try. His other two brothers were coming into town soon. They claimed they missed Max, which he believed, because Max had his own personality and they had spent time with him and appreciated him. Both confirmed bachelors, they had taken an amazing interest in his boy.

Once inside the vehicle, heat radiated all around them. The rains last night hadn't provided any relief and his dash thermostat showed ninety degrees outside. Sierra's shapely thigh next to the gear shift didn't help either.

"Wow, if I'd thought you'd drag me through a store trying stuff for three hours, I might have declined this invitation. Are we going to lasso some lunch?" he asked, trying out his best cowboy twang.

"You're in farm country, not ranch territory."

"Don't both farmers and ranchers love the land and their animals?"

She rolled her eyes. "I'll give you that." He felt his shoulders relax. He hadn't realized that the retail therapy had worked in reverse for him. But now that they were moving on, he was beginning to have fun.

She checked the time on her cell. "Now, we've got just enough time to cross a task off on the agenda before we eat."

"I can hardly wait."

She either didn't notice his sarcasm or chose to ignore it.

"Neither can I. Let's take the scenic route back to Fair Creek and skip the highway. It's so pretty here."

Chapter 24

They rode the rest of the way listening to a station that played tunes from their high school years, and chiming in on the lyrics.

Within sight of the Fair Creek town limits, she directed him. "Hang a right at the next country road." A mutt wandered out of the driveway of the house where they stopped. A black truck with huge tires with a "For Sale" sign in the window caught his eye. He adored his Beamer, the feel of the steering wheel in his hand and how the seat surrounded him. But this was different.

He realized he was staring when Sierra stood by the vehicle and he hadn't even shut off the engine. He got out and went to her.

"What do you think?" She acted like she was giving him a birthday present. In a way, she was. As a kid, he'd always carried a toy truck around in his hand.

"I think I could get used to it."

A screen door slammed and a towering man came out of the house.

"Impressive, isn't she?"

For some reason, Wyatt wished he had worn his new clothes home like Sierra had suggested. He loosened his tie. Maybe she had been right about the clothes on a man.

"Nice truck. How many miles on it?"

"Twenty thousand. Runs like a top. Would you like to drive her, take her for a spin?"

He looked at Sierra, who had the biggest grin on her face. He could feel himself smiling just as big. He'd always wanted a pickup. He didn't know why he hadn't done this sooner. Something about buying it from a good old boy seemed better than from a dealership. He'd always remember this shopping trip.

"Sure. I'll be careful."

"Don't worry too much. She's been in the mud races and you know how messy those are."

He had no idea but nodded like he understood completely.

Wyatt turned to Sierra.

"Ride with me. You got me into this."

"I'd love to."

The man handed him the key and Wyatt opened the passenger door. The place to put her foot was way up high. Sierra hoisted herself up, then seemed to lose her balance. She needed help so Wyatt wrapped his hands around her waist and boosted Sierra up onto the mammoth seat.

He reached to put his seatbelt on, and Sierra did the same. She reached up to fluff her hair, which must have been a habit for her now. It made his heart flip every time she did it.

The engine let out a roar, snapping him to reality, and he called out.

"Ready?"

"As I'll ever be."

Taking off down the road, he couldn't wipe the smile off his face. Even though the vehicles had nothing in common, driving this mondo truck reminded him of his driving around in his Mustang in high school with Sierra by his side.

At the end of the trial run, he talked the guy down a bit and paid cash for the balance.

He tossed the keys to Caleb's truck to Sierra to drive to park in front of Delaney's for Annie. He would drive his "new" truck. They arrived at the diner and he waited while she left the keys and came back and jumped in.

At a stop sign, Sierra peeked into the rearview mirror to see if her cheeks looked as flushed as they felt. She'd been needlessly concerned that Wyatt Galloway might look a little out of his element in everyday clothes. Not hardly. If anything, his attraction quotient had escalated.

Riding down Main Street beside Wyatt was the whipped cream

on top of a day as sweet as a hot fudge sundae and reminded her of cruising in the old days. And people always craned their necks to see an unfamiliar truck driving by, even though they were a dime a dozen in Fair Creek. They might as well have been in a parade from the looks they got. A child waved from the sidewalk. She shouted a bit at Wyatt to be heard over the engine, or muffler, or whatever made that revved-up sound.

"See, this is a warm, friendly town."

Wyatt rolled the window down. "Only toward a truck. And the boy is maybe age three. What does that say about them?"

She squinted for a closer look. He was right about the child. Just then, an older woman stepped out of the grocery store wearing some kind of floppy hat and all Sierra could see was a wide smile beamed directly at Wyatt.

Sierra nodded in the woman's direction to avoid pointing. "Not all of them. You've captivated that one."

He made a short, loud horn blast. "That's my Aunt Elizabeth," he said. The broad smile he flashed could have belonged to a movie star. But it was the horn that had her heart thumping. Couldn't be that she was developing a thing for him.

"Nice save. This is a kind town. Even relatives wave to one another." She put her palm to her chest. "Don't make that noise again. Be still my heart."

She sniffed the dry air and scanned the tree leaves, their edges parched and crinkled. Last night's storm barely had an impact on the summer's drought.

At the Fair Creek Community Church, a small cluster of

people were gathered. Any day of the week, something went on around here. A red pick-up with "Just Married" scrawled across the back of the cab slowly pulled away from the curb. A young woman in a full bridal gown seated in a metal folding chair in the truck bed gazed at a man in a tux jacket and jeans. Corny and sweet, the couple tugged at her heartstrings, although that most definitely wasn't for her. She needed to think about something else. She glanced over at Wyatt, and he had turned away from the couple, too.

Thankfully, the truck full of romantic dreams turned off and took her mind off what she couldn't have. While Wyatt's company had been fun today, they were not going into a relationship. She swallowed the lump in her throat.

"I'm sure you need something to drink by now," she said. "I know I do. It's so hot."

"Yeah, guess it's a good thing you're taking me home. I'll send you off with a cold drink." At the stop sign, his eyes met hers. "I've been to twenty countries, trekked the Amazon, and done relief work in Haiti. But little Fair Creek, Indiana, and my family farm, a mere dot on the map of the world, has me in its grip."

He came around and helped her climb down from her side of the truck. Did he include her in that speck of the world that gripped him? When she figured out what she wanted, maybe she would ask him.

Instead, she kept it light. "You're such a show-off," she said, teasing him.

He raised an eyebrow. "Not really."

"I think it's what the kids might call a humble brag. Look it up."

"I'm charmed by you, and Fair Creek. That has to mean something after all the places I've been? Today was more enjoyable than I thought it would be."

"Not sure if that's really a compliment." She fluffed her hair, then she stopped to think. She didn't have hearing aids in. "I was going to tell you there's an economic growth meeting two nights from now at six in the bead store. You and I will meet before then. Tomorrow night, okay?"

He removed his Stetson and smoothed his hair and her fingers itched to help. The thought hit her with a jolt. She needed to pay attention to what he said.

"Tomorrow night sounds fine. But I don't see how I can be at the bead store meeting."

She shifted her feet and tried to hide her disappointment. Maybe he wasn't as serious as she'd thought, because that meeting was the first step toward what he'd said he wanted. "I understand. I shouldn't have mentioned it."

"No. It's Max. None of his babysitters are available most nights. Aunt Elizabeth goes to her extension homemakers club. I'm out of options."

Her relief was out of proportion to the situation, but she couldn't help it. He had a real conflict.

"Bring him. We're all about building a better future, for all of us, Max included. And, I have a surprise for you. Actually, it may be more of a shock, but I hope not."

"Now you've got my full attention. What is it? Don't keep me in suspense."

"Well, I'd like to be listed as one of Max's babysitters. After the meeting, I'm inviting you to come see how I've babyproofed my apartment to welcome him. We barely know each other, in a way. But if you get in a pinch and feel like I could do a good job with him, that's what I wanted to offer."

"That's the sweetest gesture I can ever remember. Max was drawn to you from the beginning. I hoped you might want to get to know him. So a resounding 'yes,' to possibly adding you to the list. But bringing him to the meeting is a 'maybe,' especially to my first one."

"He'll be fine. These are informal."

"If you say so. We'll be there, on the condition that if he gets too restless, we can leave."

Sierra said, "That's no fair. I never get to leave when I get restless."

"Good point. He gets restless, you both can leave and I'll take over."

"Not a chance."

She had a feeling she would be the one who would have trouble paying attention. When Wyatt talked about Max being in her life, she knew they were both in the same package.

Both of them were becoming dear to her. Was that going to get her into trouble?

Chapter 25

By the time Sierra got to Delaney's the day after shopping with Wyatt, she was ready for good news. Thank goodness for Annie covering for her. She had to face it that there was no customer rush, at least not today. She felt a kick in the gut. She needed another great idea, like going to the ballpark had been. But she had to get her inventory system up first, which she intended to start on.

She entered the back door, the scent of burgers on the grill something she never tired of. One close-up look at the expression on Annie's face told her something was off. Patience wasn't Sierra's strong suit, no matter how hard she tried.

"Spill," she said.

"It's been a little crazy around here," Annie said. Her eyes seemed extra bright, like she was hyper.

Sierra's gut tightened. First, the freezer had started leaking. Amazingly, the power had not been off from the storm for so long that they had to throw anything out. Now something else today. Desperately as she wanted to keep Delaney's, she'd started to wonder if she would be able to.

"Go on. You can tell me."

Sierra looked around the empty dining room. Some of the tables could use a wipe-down and a few chairs needed straightened. But there was no evidence of anything close to the nuclear meltdown she had envisioned from Annie's attitude and slumped shoulders.

"Remember when the long-time health inspector retired, the one who Aunt Lucy said was like family and she gave him a gift card for a going away present? Well, his replacement came in today."

Sierra sucked in air, focused on her cousin now. All her fellow ice cream shop owners feared the health inspector. There was a regular feature on the subject in the association magazine.

A visit from the health department was a restaurant owner's worst nightmare. Well-managed restaurants could get write-ups for small things, like the inspectors just wanted to keep them on their toes. Greenhorn inspectors were the worst.

"And?"

"Well, it wasn't too bad, not at first. He recommended the bottles of sanitizers be moved a few inches, little things like they always pick on. Scolded us for chewing gum."

Sierra frowned. "That's new. We've never been told that."

"That's what I said, but it didn't make any difference to him, not that I could tell."

"I guess we'll survive it. But anything they point out makes us look bad."

"I agree. And it gets worse. The newspaper publisher extraordinaire happened to be in, first time ever, probably cooking up a bad review."

Sierra didn't need this. But Aunt Lucy had taught her an owner had to maintain a can-do attitude.

"Well, the newspaper covers everything related to the public anyway. It's on record. Nothing we can do about it."

"You're right. I guess it isn't the end of the world."

Sierra nodded, although this could register a body blow to her business. The health department visits were always serious, and customers read and shared them.

Annie switched gears and her gaze seemed to roam around the dining room.

"Unfortunately, we're not done yet."

"Nothing could be as bad as a surprise visit from the health inspector."

"Hold that thought because the phone's been ringing off the wall for you."

"Why?"

Annie explained that some people called about seeing her and Wyatt together, unhappy given how he'd left her at prom. "Someone tried to cancel your bringing ice cream cups for the softball tournament but I told them it was too late. That ship had already sailed with my order using your new plan." She brushed her hands together like that one was over.

"I'm missing something. Why do people care about any of this?"

"Who knows? Some are not happy they saw you with Wyatt in his truck on Main Street. They want to know if you think that's wise, given he's trying to put up those solar panels everybody's against."

"Really? I love this little town. But sometimes it just seems so . . ." She flung up her hands, searching for the right word. "Little!"

She wouldn't mention that at first she had these very same concerns about Wyatt. How could she piece together the reasons she had grown to trust him? It wasn't just one thing. His character, since she had spent time with him. How he accepted her and everything about her.

The farmer who'd sold Wyatt the truck approached them, waving the latest copy of the *Gazette*, which she hadn't read yet. What was he doing here?

Annie leaned over and murmured. "Looks like you're going to find out some issues first-hand."

His face bright red, the man's tone came out like a rant. "It was bad enough you brought him to buy my truck, which, uh, I'm glad to get the truck sold. But I reckon I might have handled it different if I'd seen this."

He slapped the newspaper onto the counter. A photo of Wyatt caught her eye and the headline, "Most residents against solar panels."

He said, "We don't want that outfit in Fair Creek. I didn't know that was him."

Sierra gathered herself up to stand taller. "If you didn't want to sell the truck to him, you shouldn't have."

Her stomach churned. What had made her think she could change peoples' opinions, especially where money was involved? Instead of influencing others to at least give Wyatt a chance, her own reputation was taking a hit.

Face it, you joined him hoping to get help with your bank loan coming due.

An image of little Max flitted through her mind. He and his dad deserved a chance in Fair Creek. She pulled herself up straighter yet.

"Wyatt Galloway's his own man, running a legitimate business that people want." She steadied her voice. "It's because he's virtually a stranger that you're not willing to listen. And did you agree with all your dad's farming practices? Farmers don't always. I'm surprised you'd be so closed-minded."

She pointed to his cap with Haven University, which taught agriculture. "I hear students are embracing change, and progress."

He opened his mouth but only spluttered. Eventually, he walked away.

Sierra's mouth dropped open, right as she felt a grip on her elbow, which then released. Startled, she looked up into Wyatt's eyes, their color as deep as the blueberry syrup in an old-fashioned Delaney's sundae. She hadn't heard him come in.

Still missing the warmth of his touch, she followed him to the dining room's back booth. "Thank you," he said. "But defending me is beyond the call of duty."

"I didn't realize how they've been treating you." Sinking into the place across from where he'd taken a seat, she realized her hands were trembling.

He brought his hand toward hers, and then stopped. Why was she disappointed? She fumbled with the sleeve of her T-shirt as he went on.

"Look, when I asked you to help, I didn't expect it to complicate your life and I'm sorry."

"I can take it." She wasn't sure, not with the health inspector debacle, but she believed in projecting confidence.

Wyatt stood, "I popped in because Max's sitter said he's fussy. I'll need to reschedule discussing the presentation this evening."

"Poor baby." She grabbed a half-empty pepper shaker from the table and stood. "I didn't tell anyone about that. I hope you'll come. My apartment is near there and I'll show you my changes for Max. You can get on the agenda for the Fair Creek Town Council. I think we can turn this around."

He shrugged. "Not sure. Maybe he's just teething."

She couldn't pull her gaze away as his back retreated toward the exit. She wasn't sure of anything.

The next day working at Delaney's went slowly for Sierra. She didn't know what tonight's meeting would hold and it played on her mind. But there wasn't any drama, either.

Finally, it was time, and her steps took her one block down to Beadangled, and the front door's bell jangled as she opened it to head inside.

"You're having way too much fun." Shirley Leap greeted her with a quick hug at the bead shop's entrance.

"Tell me about it." Sierra tacked up a sign on the door that read, "Economic Council Meets Here." After shutting the door, she went to the sofa near the worktable and plopped herself down. "What've you heard?"

Shirley started putting away beads, doodads, and tools. "Where should I start? You've been running around with the hunky Wyatt Galloway and his business has upset people. Or maybe let's start with the health department inspection violations. That sounds the juiciest."

"You know how to hurt a girl."

Her friend patted Sierra's arm where it draped over the sofa back. "I'm on your side. Can I get you anything?"

"Water sounds great."

Shirley disappeared into the curtained back room to a stocked mini fridge for visitors and her 12-year-old daughter, one of the local softball stars who was a bottomless pit and kept her widowed mom busy.

Seconds later, Shirley tossed a bottle into her palm and the fluid quenched her parched throat. "Now tell me."

"The health department cited routine violations and the new inspector wants to start out tough."

Shirley cradled her mug between her fingers, each one with a ring made of beads, and took a sip. "Most people won't see what he's up to."

"Yeah, and Alice from the newspaper happened to be in eating lunch, a first, and isn't one of my fans."

"You're having bad luck with that newspaper."

Sierra checked her cell phone for the time. "The meeting starts soon, so I'll have to answer the other stuff later."

Shirley stood brushed off he table with a cloth. "You're smooth."

Sierra glanced out the window and fluffed her hair. "The Man of the Hour approaches."

Shirley rolled her eyes and trotted toward the door. "What? Most people would be avoiding him. You have a rebel streak." She threw open the door. "Hello, Wyatt. It's a pleasure to see you again after all these years."

Wyatt stepped inside, looking more polished than any of Shirley's beads. "Thanks. Meet my little buddy."

Shirley's entire face lit up and she pretended to shake Max's hand. He gurgled.

Wyatt wore a suit she hadn't seen before, and her heart cheered. He was such his own person, and with Max on one hip and the cloth fold-up stroller tucked under his elbow, her. mouth went dry.

Sierra hurried to take an excited, kicking Max from Wyatt's arms. She inhaled his sweet, soapy scent while trying to ignore the heat from brushing against his father's arm. A spicy aftershave wafted up.

Focus.

Wyatt helped her strap Max into his stroller where he chewed on a set of plastic keys in primary colors. With a jingle, the door opened and Marv and Trudy, who were farmers, stepped in. Ted Mitchell followed them, and her regulars who came in for coffee every morning filed in behind him.

Ted caught Sierra's eye. "May we join you?"

Sierra opened her water bottle and gulped a swig. "Of course." They all took seats around the large table, with Wyatt beside her, and she began.

"Last month's meeting attendance: Sierra Delaney. New business—"

"That was the attendance? Just you?" Wyatt interrupted her.

She felt her face flush. "When I told you our economic council was just getting started. Would you mind introducing yourself?"

His fingers touched his Stetson. "Wyatt Galloway. Businessowner and farmer."

The others nodded, although Marv and Trudy exchanged a look, not smiling.

Ted spoke. "We represent numerous others who are against bringing solar here. We respect your family, though."

Hoping to head off discussion, she regrouped. "I appreciate your coming. Mr. Galloway's giving a presentation at the next Fair Creek Town Council meeting. Hope you'll join us."

"Please call me Wyatt like everybody else does, as far as I know."

Some chuckles sounded and Sierra exhaled. Her list of topics was limited. Max tossed his keys to the floor and squawked. Wyatt stood, unstrapped him, and walked around the room. Sierra swallowed. He needed to sit and a baby crawling around might find a bead or worse.

She held out her arms and Wyatt let the baby come into them before sitting down. Discussion continued but when he squirmed, Sierra set Max's diaper-padded rear on the table and played makeshift pattycake.

Shirley pulled stray box of beads to her and closed it with a click. "We'll need to figure out our assets and highlight them. Great meeting. Let's adjourn." She picked up Sierra's gavel and rapped it on the table.

In less than ten minutes, Sierra and Wyatt had regrouped and arrived at the old building she lived in. Wyatt, with Max in his arms, walked side by side with Sierra up the staircases to her third-floor apartment. A closeness remained, maybe from their united front at the meeting.

She held onto the banister, and patted Max's leg with her other hand as they went. "I might be premature, but I feel hopeful."

"Let's talk about it tomorrow and focus on Max now."

Her stomach fluttered, at this homier version. She unlocked her door and went inside.

He came into the entry way and kept Max in his arms, then stooped down to what would be his son's eye level. The child was walking some, but not real steady on his feet for more than a couple of steps.

Sierra's stomach knotted as Wyatt went through and checked what she'd done based on her internet search. Her outlets all had plastic plugs in them to protect little fingers. Her decorating style, if you could call it that, was sparse. However, she'd moved her glassware, all family heirlooms, into high cabinets.

Wyatt said nothing, intent on looking everywhere. She had plastic locks so the lower cabinets couldn't be opened. She'd left out one of her metal pans with a lid in the kitchen. Max squirmed in his daddy's arms and when Wyatt sat him down, his chubby hand found them. Thankfully, her hearing aids weren't in.

Wyatt's smile at Max faded as the racket increased, and within seconds, he'd pulled Max away.

The three of them moved through the rooms. When Wyatt stopped, dropped to his knees, and dragged a box of paper clips on the floor from under the coverlet's edge, her heart sank.

Wyatt's eyes gave nothing away.

Heart thumping, she plucked the little box away. "I've baby-proofed. But he won't be on his own—ever."

The corners of his mouth tweaked up. "He's quick. Don't ask me how I know."

As if on cue, Max squealed at a small, stuffed raccoon. Wyatt set him down where he could toddle to it.

With the child occupied, their eyes met and locked. Wyatt's had gold flecks, encircled by dark brown, and held all kinds of stories she longed to know and never would. As though frozen in place, they continued to look at one another.

He waved his hand through the air. "Thank you for this, and

the raccoon's perfect."

Coming from him, she was warmed all over. "I wanted him to have something of his own when he comes to visit."

Wyatt's engaging smile was life itself. The stubble above his upper lip sent flutters to her stomach. "You've thought of everything."

Except how to spend time with Max and his daddy, knowing she couldn't make a forever home with them.

Or could she?

Chapter 26

The hearing aids were finally in and Sierra finished what she was doing at Delaney's. Wyatt pulled to the curb and picked her up. She hadn't wanted him to go to her doctor's appointment with her to get her hearing aids programmed to wear, but Wyatt had insisted he needed to go back to the get some special candy for the kids. He could give it away at the July Fourth community party.

She suspected some of the urgency he had created was made up. In the end, she decided she would enjoy the company. Now that he knew about her hearing aids, and since he worked so closely with her, she felt relaxed around him. She'd also fallen for him more and more. But once she began wearing them full time, she figured their chemistry would change. No matter what he told her, who wanted technology around their ears? Or their significant others' ears, or wanted to maneuver around the plastic. Or maybe that was just her since she was not a fan.

She sure would appreciate the boost in sounds, though. Shoving all the thoughts aside, she climbed into the truck, and they rode in companiable silence.

She stared out the window at the houses, which became more plentiful as they came closer to the city. She said he could drop her off but he insisted on parking and escorting her into the building. Then he left to get candy at the specialty story on the circle.

Wyatt realized a sense of dread about Sierra getting her hearing aids back. It felt like an unknown in their relationship. He had been working side by side with her at the diner and was going to miss that. He didn't know what to expect and she was keyed up about the change. Since Sadie had shown what kind of damage she could do to the expensive things, he wanted to be extra cautious.

Once his candy errand was done, he randomly popped into a little shop and ended up picking out a small gift for Sierra.

He then found her back at the doctor's office. She looked up, her eyes sparkling, which he took as a very good sign. She went to him and gave him a peck on the cheek. "How did it go with the candy?"

"Fine. Got everything I wanted. It was fun."

They left and waited to ride the elevator. He didn't know whether to ask the obvious or not.

"How are they working?"

Her cheeks flushed. "Great." Then she shrugged. "Right now, things seem extra loud. You'd think that would be good. But it's a little disorienting. I'll need to get used to them. I can't thank you enough for making this possible."

"Remember, I'm to blame that you needed new ones at all. But if this had to happen, I'm glad it worked out to your advantage."

The elevator doors opened.

They got inside with a woman who appeared a few years younger than Sierra with short, spiked hair. Her hearing aids were in plain view and she smiled at Wyatt. The doors closed and the elevator moved forward.

"Do either of you have any interest in getting massages? Most people find them super relaxing." Before he could answer, Sierra did.

"We're not from the city. So I don't think we'd be interested, but thanks."

Wyatt felt that the woman had brought in two new situations. One, was it common to be approached on an elevator for business? He didn't know if it was real. Or was she flirting with him?

And she seemed completely unconcerned about wearing hearing aids in both ears, plain to see. Not surprising to see patients, really, since they were in a medical facility.

"I've had a few massages and found them quite relaxing. But as Sierra said, we're not from around here."

Her smile at their comments oozed confidence. She gave off the vibe that if you rejected her work, or whatever else she might be promoting, she would move on without a second thought. You were the one missing out, not her.

When they reached the next floor, the woman handed him her business card. "Massage therapist," she said. "If anything changes, look me up. Thanks."

He walked out with her together, the three of them, and when the woman was out of sight, he tossed the card in the trash, clearly in Sierra's view. He wasn't sure why it mattered that she know or if it mattered, but he wasn't taking any chances.

On the way home, Sierra's mind tumbled full of thoughts. The woman in the elevator had taught her some things, about confidence and beauty. She'd been so sure of herself with Wyatt. She glanced at his profile and her heart squeezed. She hated to admit, even to herself, how jealous she was of the minor incident.

Wyatt didn't talk either, apparently lost in his own thoughts. She wasn't sure how she would do with her new hearing aids that were a different style. The audiologist had said the speakers might need to be readjusted more than once as they got them programmed correctly for her. They came with a brochure, but she hated reading directions of any kind. So she had searched for tips online.

She'd been looking forward so much to getting the gadgets

that she hadn't thought of the downside. How would she adjust when the rules kept changing?

For one thing, she hadn't been wearing anything in her ears for a while, which might not seem like much. But the doctor had told her that her brain had likely already adapted to not having the hearing aids again. Everything sounded loud now—too loud.

Wyatt turned on the turn signal. The blinking sound was funny, it was so loud. Leaves had gotten on the windshield where they parked and were stuck in the hood grate. He turned the windshield wipers on to clear off some leaves. Scrape. Scrape. Scrape. That was also too loud.

But she couldn't wait to try them out at Delaney's, to be among her customers.

Chapter 27

Wyatt continued to navigate the roads back from the doctor's office to Fair Creek, as Sierra adjusted to her new hearing aids. Talking to her, as hard as it was, had helped him to sort things out. He felt compelled to tell her more about Bethany. He felt better getting it off his chest and it might help her to understand some of his actions. Maybe she would open up more to him too.

"You know, I normally don't share any details about Bethany and me. I have told you she manipulated me and was not faithful to me. But the way all this happened also made it difficult. She died several hours after Max's birth, of a heart condition they didn't know she had. Our relationship hadn't been good, but we were going to work together for our new baby's sake."

Sierra's expression showed concern, and she spoke softly,

with compassion. "I can see how hard that would be."

"I was devastated by her death and didn't know which way was up, what with caring for a newborn and missing her." His hand gripped the wheel and Sierra looked at him. "My best friend stayed right along beside me through it all, which made the situation almost bearable. Until I realized the reason for his motivations. He had loved her, too. They'd been having an affair. She tried to cut it off when she became pregnant with Max but they remained emotionally connected throughout the pregnancy."

"Wyatt, now that you've said that, I'm piecing some things together. For a short time, I dated someone who had little in common with me. I'd been having trouble finding anyone I wanted to date. And, honestly, as my hearing worsened, some struggles I had at restaurants and other places had me asking, 'why bother?' I became a bit of a hermit."

"You're so pretty and so great in so many ways. I can't believe any of that would happen to you. But I feel for you. We can all get in relationships that aren't good for us."

She nodded. "It's true. And we know God has a plan. That plan also includes all of our relationships. But I feel like for myself, I had taken things into my own hands. When I met the guy, I was not as particular as I would normally have been. Guess I was lonely, plain and simple."

They pulled up to the Fair Creek stop sign. When there were no vehicles around, Wyatt glanced over, and her deep green eyes captivated him. He said, "I value your friendship, Sierra. Thank you for being a good listener. You give me hope."

He reached into his pocket and presented her with a tiny bag. "Whatever happens, we'll always be connected."

Sierra couldn't believe Wyatt had found the cute little horses that dangled from such delicate earrings. "You shouldn't have. I'll treasure them forever."

She released the jewelry from their thin cardboard holder. This morning there had been no time for earrings.

Wyatt leaned forward, his dark brown eyes studying her. Their lips met. Sweet and tender, he tasted like sugar and a tinge of something spicey. She melted when he reached in and touched her cheek. With his other hand he picked up the earrings in her palm. When he moved toward her ears, she didn't want to, but she stiffened.

Maybe he would just ignore her ears and what was behind them. But his strong, gentle fingers continued upward. He whispered in her ear. "I appreciate all of you. If I'm careful, may I help with your earrings?"

That rich, low voice—one gift the hearing aids gave her. She swallowed the lump in her throat. "Okay—"

"Communicating with you is one of my favorite things. And hearing aids help so I can only be grateful."

A peace came over her.

She drew back a fraction of an inch. "Thank you, for

everything. You've been so kind not to make me feel bad about my feelings, not to push."

"Everyone's unique and has value in God's eyes. That means everything about each of us was meant to be." He lightly rested his forehead against hers and Sierra's eyes closed, as she listened. "You would have figured it out yourself. If I helped, then I'm glad."

"You've been there for me. I was coming to this conclusion. It just took time."

Back at Delaney's, she couldn't wait to try out the new hearing aids. She walked in and started talking with Annie, trying to slow her heartbeat after kissing Wyatt goodbye.

"Sorry I was gone so long. How have you managed?"

"Just fine. And that's the sad part." The sound of Annie's voice was so different. She should have expected hearing aids to seem odd after being without them.

"It's the ideal day for ice cream. I was hoping people might feel good and come out."

"Me too but that isn't what has happened so far."

"We came through a different way due to a detour because of a bridge that was out. Wonder if that impacts anything." Sierra could hear Annie's voice well and the volume was much better, but she found understanding distinct words a challenge.

"That's worth looking into. Rerouting can be such a simple

thing but people don't like the hassle. I'll check to be sure the detour signs are clearly marked. Maybe I could get special permission to put up a small arrow pointing the way to Delaney's. Oh, and the health inspector's report is in today's *Gazette*."

The air whooshed out of Sierra's lungs.

Mr. Peterson the banker had come in.

The tension in her chest threatened to implode. She smiled as best she could. "Thanks for stopping by. What can I get you?"

He dropped the *Gazette* onto the counter. "A double chocolate chip shake would hit the spot about now. Your aunt used to make those with triple chocolate for me." She knew from past conversations, years ago with her aunt, that he pronounced "aunt" like it started with "ah" when the doctor wanted to examine her throat.

Fortunately, she knew what her aunt had made for him. Aunt Lucy's mind had been like a computer at keeping track of people's orders. She must have known hundreds, at least.

"A triple chocolate shake coming right up."

By the time she had finished making it, the knot in her gut was thicker than the hot fudge she had scooped on top. Bankers didn't visit for no reason, not in her world. She took his money and returned the change and started to turn away, trying to look like she had something urgent to do.

"There's something else. Don't let what came out in the *Gazette* get you down." He looked around as though he didn't want anyone else to hear. "That loan that's due at the end of the month? I'm going to modify it with you, if you're willing." His intention came out loud and clear. "I've been watching your business and it seems to be on the upturn, working with Galloway Farms, and going to the ballpark. You're a positive influence in this town and I'll partner with you to continue by extending the loan."

"I'm very interested and appreciate the chance to continue."
Thank you, Lord.

Chapter 28

Just twenty-four hours with the hearing aids had made a difference. After a hectic day at Delaney's, Sierra's heartbeat had settled by the time she stood on Wyatt's front porch. Soft music drifted through the screen door. Sweet yet melancholy, a clear male voice that had to be Wyatt, rang through, accompanied by a guitar. The melody stirred a longing that rooted her in place. The music stopped and she knocked so she wouldn't interrupt him in the middle of a song.

He answered the door and Wyatt looked scrumptious, barefoot in jeans and a T-shirt, a guitar hanging at his hip.

He glanced down at her, and then leaned down for a kiss. The delicious feel of his lips on hers would never get old. She tasted coffee and reached up to run her fingers through the hair at the nape of his neck.

When they pulled away, he said, "Hello."

"I've missed you," she said as they moved into the room.

Part of her hearing problems had impacted how she felt about music. She'd always liked the music on the radio, and when in band at school, she'd gone to concerts. She had always been a goner for a guy with a guitar, or trumpet, or piano, for that matter. His black T-shirt, the letters spelling Born Free, Taxed to Death, made the hue of his eyes even darker brown. The short sleeves clearly showed his toned biceps. Her pulse kicked up a notch–or five. With a slow intake of breath, she reminded herself for the umpteenth time to focus on business.

Yeah, right.

His guitar playing must have softened him too.

"Welcome to our pad. Max had trouble settling to sleep so I played for him. He made an early night of it and is asleep in bed."

He motioned her inside, starting to pull the guitar strap over his head.

"Please, don't stop on my account. May I set this down somewhere?"

When he nodded, she set a large bowl of chicken and noodles she'd had leftover on a potholder on the glass tabletop nearby.

He patted the guitar. "Getting this baby out takes me back to college, once I got to go. That was when picking the best pizza on a Friday night was the biggest decision. Sometimes I miss that."

He tilted his head slightly and appeared to consider her request, the guitar in one hand, the strap dangling.

"Are you sure you want me to play? I've inconvenienced you

enough already by asking you to come back to my home," he said, glancing over the fireplace at a mounted deer.

"Um, I've looked forward to this all day. I have a soft spot for Galloway Sons Farm, honestly. And especially for you and Max," she smiled. "He's better off here in his own bed. I could have said no. Please, play some more."

He cradled the instrument closer. "If you insist."

He sat down at one end of the sectional, and she gave him room to play, by taking on the center section. She put a file with her jottings on a table next to her. Wyatt strummed a short introduction and the first note he sang had a hushed, almost reverent quality. They were so close that it was like he was speaking directly to her. Singing only for her. The intimacy made her heart rate kick up.

Her digital hearing aids messed up sometimes, but she enjoyed the sounds. The softness of his voice and the gentle way he strummed the guitar allowed her to hear most detail, and she held her breath from listening so intently. At his soulful expression, her mouth went dry.

Wrapped up in the moment, Sierra slipped off her sandals, pulled her knees up, and hugged them to her chest, where her heart pounded. He sang an especially tender low note, and let it fade to end the song. Something in her wanted to weep for the loss but she put her hands together to softly clap her appreciation.

"Please." He waved her off and stood up. "I'm an amateur." He removed the strap from around his neck and placed his instrument in a stand.

"That was so special." She sighed.

They moved into the kitchen where its green-checked café curtains reminded her of her mother's kitchen, when Sierra was growing up. "Whatever you're making smells wonderful." She inhaled. "I love to sample other people's cooking." Sadie slunk in with a toy mouse in her mouth and they gave each other the side eye before she left.

"Don't get your hopes up. Somebody left a grill on the back deck or I might have starved to death. Having so many brothers milling around has its advantages. Fortunately, I can grill a mean steak, so I'll never go hungry."

"Yum. Thank goodness my efforts at becoming a vegetarian have stalled. So there's some truth to the nickname, 'The Amazing Galloway Sons,' huh? I've met Caleb and heard of Gage. Who's the other one?"

"Leo. My oldest brother is difficult to describe. He got all the artistic genes. Poor guy."

"I'm not buying that. I really did enjoy your guitar strumming."

"Well, thanks. Business is what makes me tick, though."

Knowing he wasn't a gourmet chef had lifted her spirits. She loved guys who cooked, as long as their skills didn't exceed hers, which were more home cooking than gourmet.

Focus, Sierra.

This was her show to run, learning about his business. "Let's get started, why don't we?"

"Sounds good, I'd like to move in to the table in the dining area, so we'll have room for your papers and I can keep an eye on the grill. Let me bring Max's baby monitor."

Sierra settled into a big, wood chair with upholstered seat and he took one across from her. "I've researched what people are most concerned about in town," she said. "The translation of what 'research' means? I talked with the group of regulars that come in for coffee every day."

Wyatt grinned. "I love it. You are the perfect person for this. Let me say that I've analyzed every angle and there really are no new concerns that people have. But some areas focus on one more than another. So this will really help."

She rifled through her papers once, then again, tried to find what she wanted and focus. "Oh, here it is." She held up a dinner napkin and menu. "Sorry but these were handy when I talked to the guys. I'm happy to say that business has been picking up."

"Hey, whatever works. This is grass roots information and I'm grateful."

She studied the napkin. "Okay, one of the main concerns is how the neighbors' property values might go down. They don't think they look good."

"Yes, that's a common one. It's not the easiest to battle, but it's all what everyone is used to. I mean, a great big tractor isn't that attractive either. But we've normalized that. I mean, farmers actually admire one another's tractors. In the research I've done, and the follow-up studies, people stop even noting the panels are there in three months' time or less."

Sitting near him like this, while he shared ideas he was clearly passionate about, eyes sparkling as he made his point, she had hope. Maybe he could convince the townspeople.

He went to the refrigerator, grabbed out two bottles of water, and handed her one. For the next hour, they went on, with her covering the concerns, then him addressing each one in a compelling way. In between, he worked on the simple meal.

Finally, she finished the list and sat back in her chair. "You've done extremely well, with just the right touch of emotion and facts. You might have a chance. I'm not only going to help get this information out but will be happy to do it."

"You think so?"

"Now, don't get me wrong. This may be one of your toughest crowds, so you'll want to be on your game, to be listening carefully."

"Yes, I'm constantly reminding myself of that at presentations. It's what they perceive to be the problem that really matters."

She opened her notebook. "Now, they've got a campaign going with those signs. It's time you counteract that. Let's go over your strongest arguments, compress them into bite-sized pieces. I'll order them as signs. Put some up in Delaney's, and you can see if any others will too. I'll give you names of people to talk with."

He nodded, and they worked together deciding what the best phrases were.

This had been very intense. One of her knees started twitching but it was under the table so he wouldn't notice. Just outside the sliding door, steam billowed from the grill. "You might want to check your meat."

He jumped up, grabbed a plate and set of tongs from the counter and arrived out at the grill in three long strides. He carried in two steaks and the scent nearly made her swoon. It was the steaks and not the way he wielded the grill utensils nor the way his biceps flexed under the T-shirt. Definitely not.

"I hope you like medium rare," he said. He quirked an eyebrow and could have won an award for the most handsome grill master Sierra had ever seen. She swallowed like he wasn't affecting her.

"Is there any other kind?" She let out a nervous giggle in relief. "What can I do to help?"

He assured her he had everything under control and in minutes, they began eating.

"Tell me how you got into this line of work," she said, leaning back in the chair. Having a guy talk about his job was always safe territory. Sitting so close had her heartbeat galloping. She could easily reach over and touch a curl that had fallen down on his forehead.

"What drew you to solar?"

He thought for a minute, as though sorting through what he wanted to say. "From the minute I heard about it at this special presentation at Miles' school, I felt connected to it. I mean, energy runs everything. An alternative energy that had never been utilized in any great degree? Even better."

He was off on all the ways he loved solar, and Sierra thought she might fall in love with it too, based on his own personal energy. When he finished, he gulped some water.

"That was outstanding."

"Honestly, I've had a lot of people react that way. I've honed my own story about how I got into it, as part of the narrative. But I feel I need to give you a little bit more. Just so you understand."

Afterward, he insisted on handling the dishes himself, stacking them into the dishwasher. Max hadn't made a peep. She brought in the grilling tools and rinsed them. She finished, her thoughts only on him the entire time.

Later, as she went out the door with his kisses on her lips, she thought maybe she wasn't falling in love with solar at all. But maybe with the guy behind the ideas.

Chapter 29

The next morning, Sierra drove out to the farm, trying to keep her nervous energy at bay. Something about working with Wyatt on ideas for solar had reminded her of something. She probably should have called first. But if he wasn't there or it was not good timing, he would tell her. She looked out at the sunshine on the soybean fields and hummed, *This Little Light of Mine.*

She parked and found Wyatt in a new office he'd made in the barn. "Hey, hope it's okay that I dropped in? I've got a marketing idea to run by you."

He closed his computer.

"It's more than okay."

Nerves set in so she walked over and looked out of the window. Louise was eating grass under a tree.

"I've been mulling something for a while and I'd like for you to know about it," she said. "Once our ad agency worked with a visitors bureau. They had made a chocolate trail, where visitors to town followed this map and found treasure kind-of-thing."

Wyatt came up behind her and wrapped his arms around her waist. Her heart raced, but her nerves had settled and she could breathe again.

"What's that supposed to mean? Like Hansel and Gretel's crumbs only with Hershey bars?"

"Close, but not exactly. All of the businesses in town came up with chocolate items. Visitors would get a passport stamped and a treat for going to each of the locations—like a candle store had a chocolate candle and, of course, some of the places were actually chocolate stores."

"I don't follow. What does this have to do with Fair Creek?"

"Well, for a tiny place, we have some nice businesses. Rather than struggling separately to make it, how can we work together? Play up our assets?"

"I really like the sound of that."

She turned around to face him. He leaned down and kissed her. It seemed so natural when he touched her hair, and her hearing aids didn't whistle. They had learned together how to navigate them. His firm lips tasted delicious, like cinnamon. When he drew her closer and nuzzled her neck, she thought she might sink right onto the wooden floor. Finally, they both managed to untangle themselves.

His look had so much affection and understanding, she was

warmed all over again. "Now, what were you saying?"

"Well, I don't have it all thought out. But what do you think? Maybe we could present together. Solar impacts everything and businesses need customers."

"I think it sounds wonderful. Do you think the others would go for it? Some people don't like to give away treasures and think it's not a good way to make money."

"True, but the samples wouldn't need to be large. On the chocolate trail, some were fun-sized, like the candles were votives. You got maybe a small piece. The point was to get someone into the stores, who would be interested in the other items they had. Plus, maybe they would come back. Some of them gave ice cream but that wasn't the main item. The freebie was simply a gift for giving the business a try."

"Do you think this could work?"

"It's hard to say unless we try it. The town that did it wasn't sure either. But it took off. When you look at it, there's very little investment involved. A bakery could have a bite-sized brownie sample. We'd have to try it, give it a fair shake. That town tripled their expectations for the first year. Then it steadily grew."

They spent some time talking about how to introduce the concept at the next town council meeting.

Finally, Sierra was ready to leave. Wyatt walked her to her van and she got in and powered the window down. "I'm so glad you came." He leaned down for another kiss. "Max will be sad he missed seeing you."

She could get lost in his eyes. "Give him an extra snuggle for me when he wakes up. And Wyatt, I'm really glad I came too. The next council meeting is in two days, so I'll have more reasons to see you."

"Can you stop, just for a moment?"

She pulled back, slightly alarmed. "What's that supposed to mean?"

"I'm done talking business."

Sierra's heartbeat kicked up and she spoke softly. "I'm always open to changing topics, Mr. Galloway."

"Oh, I'm afraid I've misled you, Ms. Delaney. I don't want to talk at all." He leaned into the van window and looked into her eyes, inches from her. "Thank you for a terrific evening. It's been great, because I've spent it with you. Can you think of anything else we could do together?"

She closed the gap, and the warm pressure of his lips made her wonder why they'd talked at all. Wrapping her hands around his neck, she let him take the lead. The intensity took her breath.

A chirp came over the baby monitor. Wyatt moaned, reluctantly pulling away.

She said, "You're right. We've been talking about business way too much."

Chapter 30

The Fair Creek Town Council meeting started on time and Wyatt didn't know what would happen, a situation he had always hated. He and Sierra had hammered out the details, which had taken a lot of time together. That had suited him fine. They had gotten approved to be co-presenters.

After the pledge, he waited through all the usual town business and then their names were called. She came around the table to his side as they'd agreed to show solidarity.

"I'm excited to share the latest idea for promoting the town and surrounding areas," she said, reminding him of the time she had led the senate when they were in school. She was a natural leader.

"What's a town's goal when a customer comes into town?" She paused and glanced at the table where each board member sat with their names on a marker in front of them.

"Keep them here as long as possible and entice them into visiting as many businesses as possible. That's what!" She beamed a bright smile around the room.

Wyatt stepped into place next to her, unable to ignore the sweet, clean scent of her that wafted over to him. "What's a way to entice folks to stay?" He paused to let that sink in. "In a world where fun and games rules, we make coming to town into a game."

A couple of board members sat up a little bit in their seats. The others remained leaned back and looked skeptically at him. Raised eyebrows told him they weren't sure. Some doodled on their pads. He proceeded to explain how the Chocolate Trail would work. When he had finished, he opened the floor for questions.

An elderly member at the far corner of the table asked a question which he thought was perfect for Sierra. She addressed it. Then he took the next one. They kept the time to a minimum. He was next.

The board had a discussion among themselves and the measure to explore the possibility of a Chocolate Trail passed four to one.

Next Sierra introduced him for an opening statement.

"Wyatt Galloway comes from a family whose name most of us know. What many don't know is that Wyatt became excited about solar energy from a young age. I've seen his presentation and he has information we should all listen to. Fair Creek is a fantastic little town and we all want to keep it that way. But there are waves of the future that we need to consider. Please welcome Wyatt, founder and CEO of Vortex Clean Energy."

A patter of quiet claps drew his attention and Ted Mitchell and his buddies sat in the back row. "Thank you, Sierra and thanks to the board for giving me a chance to share tonight. Let me start by saying that I've listened to what you've said. I've seen the signs. I'll ask you to do the same.

"Also, Turner County, one of your neighbors, has just issued a county solar ordinance. After months of negotiations and public discussion, they have a plan that both sides can live with. Let me explain. They went through five drafts. One of the concerns is keeping those who don't want solar panels distanced from those who do. Many counties only require a 300-feet setback. But Turner County put in place a 1,320-feet setback. All I'm asking tonight is to set up public meetings and address the concerns. Maybe those will result in an ordinance and maybe they won't. That will be up to you and the citizens of Fair Creek."

Wyatt sat down and waited for the vote. After the discussion, the vote came in at three to two for taking the process forward.

Outside in the hallway afterward, Wyatt went up to Sierra who was surrounded by board members. She pulled away from the group.

She brushed his hand briefly, since they'd agreed to keep things professional. "Congratulations on bringing solar energy to Fair Creek."

"And you did well in there, too."

"Going through all of the questions you asked me and concerns you came up with strengthened my presentation."

"We make a good team. We have always worked well together."

Sierra stayed to schmooze with her "regulars," and Wyatt needed to get home to Max. On the drive to Galloway Sons Farm, he couldn't help but wonder what the future held. He only knew that he wanted her in it. His worries about leading Max into an unhealthy relationship didn't apply to Sierra. Not at all.

Chapter 31

"Aunt Sierra!–Aunt Sierra!" Chloe shrieked as Sierra headed toward the gazebo across the street from her apartment building. She had invited the Galloways who were going to the parade to meet there and walk to the little downtown. Sierra stooped down as the child's arms came around her neck.

"Happy July Fourth, sweetie. This is just about my favorite holiday."

"Mine too!"

After Sierra had untangled herself from the hug, a male voice boomed out above her head. "Good morning, Sierra."

She gave Wyatt a goofy grin. "Good morning to you. I didn't expect to see you until later."

They just stood and smiled at each other, and she was pretty sure they both had on exaggerated cartoon smiles. He wore a dark-navy T-shirt with the holiday stamped on it and she did, too.

"I'm so glad you thought of getting the shirts."

Sierra said, "You all will make quite the display on Main Street. I'm not going to take all the blame for this."

Wyatt said, "We both made it happen. If people think we're obnoxious, I'll deny everything."

"But seriously, what happened to your plans to ride in the parade?"

"I wanted to be here with Max and with you. Aunt Elizabeth gave me a pass for sending our horse trainer for Galloway Sons Farm, riding on Louise. Some things are just more important than looking good on a horse." He gave her a kiss and a warm hug and she leaned in for more.

"Now, don't forget there are children here, guys." They pulled away to see Caleb standing beside them. The brothers exchanged morning greetings and did the slapping on the back that men liked.

Caleb pulled over a sturdy wooden wagon with red slats he placed on the gazebo's floor. Annie tucked Ella and Drew inside, and Sierra and Chloe helped surround them with blankets. Another wagon appeared for Chloe and Max to ride in, only until she got on the softball float.

"Those wagons have been around so long that Caleb and I rode in them," Wyatt said with a laugh.

The adults exchanged greetings and their little caravan

headed out toward the parade route to look for a good spot to see the parade. Fair Creek's downtown streets were blocked off for the parade so they had decided to walk. With Wyatt strolling beside her, Sierra couldn't stop smiling.

People were lined up along the route, settled in waiting for when the parade would begin. Some porches were crowded with people. Others had their front yards full of people in lawn chairs. This was the holiday of the year for Fair Creek, other than Christmas. They made the most of it. Lots of people knew Sierra from the diner and called out her name. She was adjusting to the new hearing aids.

But it was still loud and she didn't catch everything. She and Wyatt walked hand in hand. If she didn't hear someone call out her name, Wyatt squeezed her hand for a moment and nodded in the direction of the caller so she could acknowledge them.

Their little party paused at a stop sign before crossing the street.

Sierra looked at Wyatt. "I'm convinced if they had a contest for 'Who wore it best,' you would win hands down." The shirt complemented his dark-brown eyes, that were focused fully on her right now.

"You look pretty cute in yours, Ms. Delaney."

Leaning in extra close so she didn't have to shout, she said, "Thanks for letting me be an honorary Galloway for a day."

His smile crinkled the corners of his eyes. "Sounds like a reality TV show. You can be one as long as you want to." A happy shiver went up her spine.

The sidewalks were old and overgrown tree roots had pushed them into crooked shapes. Any time they came across an especially rocky place, Wyatt rested his hand on the small of her back, to steady her. She'd always wanted to feel secure and with Wyatt, she did.

When they reached Main Street, the US flags and hero banners with veterans' names and faces looked so great she might have teared up. And walking by Delaney's proved even more of a challenge to hold it together.

"Aunt Lucy would have loved this so much," Sierra said. Especially seeing Sierra with someone who cared so deeply for her. In the early years, the two of them stood outside the diner and sold snickerdoodles for half price.

"In a way, she'll be here, in spirit, along with her recipes. Can't wait to taste what you've prepared for us," Wyatt said, wrapping her hand in his.

"Aunt Lucy taught me all her secrets and I called in a bunch of favors to get so much food done so quickly."

"I envy you sometimes. Cooking is so fundamental and nurturing. And I think the way you have of serving people means a lot to so many."

"That's sweet of you to say. Honestly, I was up most of the night making sure everything was on track. But I couldn't miss the parade." *So glad you decided to walk with me.*

An hour before the parade was to start, they were able to find a nice big space on the main turn of the parade route and set up their lawn chairs. They put cowboy hats on the little ones to protect them from the sun. By then, Chloe had gone to ride on the softball team's float.

At exactly noon, the fire truck sirens went off signaling the start of the parade. Floats and clowns went by, with people tossing out candy everywhere. The littles abandoned their wagons and the adults supervised while excessive amounts of candy were tossed, which wouldn't be consumed by children.

Sierra relaxed as the day wore on and a few council members actually walked by and stopped to shake Wyatt's hand.

When the fire trucks went by, one of the firefighters called out to him.

"Hey, with your build, you'd make a great volunteer fireman."

"Maybe I'll consider that then. Thanks!"

"We'll put you in our annual calendar." The truck moved on by before he could answer, if he even wanted to.

Aunt Elizabeth helped the babies and then surprised Sierra by standing up. She followed where Elizabeth was looking. The regulars at the diner had created their own float in the shape of a teacup. They'd even put "Delaney's" on the side.

Ted tossed candy to the crowd, and unless she was mistaken, he sent some Elizabeth's way intentionally. Even from a distance, Sierra could see that her eyes twinkled, and her hand was positioned in an attractive pose, like she thought he might be paying attention.

Or maybe Sierra just saw love in the air everywhere, since she had Wyatt on her mind. He was leaned over Max but caught her eye as she watched the older couple, and he winked at her.

She laughed and blew him a kiss. Her heart melted just thinking that maybe they would spend their old age together. She really had been nipped by love.

Too soon, the parade ended and the crowd began to leave. Wyatt carried Max in his arms and leaned into Sierra. "Before we get to the farm, Max and I wanted to ask you something."

She tweaked the baby's leg. "Really, Maxie? Are you talking now too?"

Wyatt kissed Max's cheek, then gestured over to a gigantic oak tree where no one was around. "I know you might not be prepared for this. But when something is right, I know it. When I started Vortex Clean Energy, I knew. Although this is way more important than anything I've ever done."

She held her breath. He seemed so serious.

He held her hand, and the warmth caused her heartbeat to pick up. "These past few weeks have been the best of my life. I have been looking for something all of my life. I didn't know what. It turned out to be someone. That someone is you."

Her heart was beating out of her chest. "Wyatt, you know I love you. But could you be happy in a small town? Your happiness is all that matters to me."

"I don't care where I am, as long as it's with you and with Max. I look at all these faces and know that I can't ever truly compete with what you have here. There is a solidarity in Fair Creek that is built over years of dedication to one another."

"Your business is valuable, too, and they might turn your business out, and then what?" she said.

"I'd give up solar panels in all fifty states for you."

"You would?" Her pulse picked up speed.

"In a heartbeat. Other than my faith, nothing is as important to me as you are."

He looked into her eyes. She wanted to believe him, more than anything she had ever wanted in her life.

"But, I know how you've always hated to lose in business."

"That, if it ever happened, would never compare to the pain of losing you, like I did before."

He got down on one knee and Max giggled. "Say you'll marry me, Sierra."

"Wyatt, I can't imagine anything I'd rather do."

He stood up, wrapped his arms around her and Max, too. "I don't ever want to be without you again," he said.

She put her answer into their kiss. It was wonderful and sweet and held the promise of a lifetime of love.

Want more stories about the Galloway Sons of Fair Creek?
Read the next book in the series:
Her Billionaire Cowboy's Triplets: Galloway Sons Farm
(Christmas in Fair Creek, Book 2)

About the Author

Cathy Shouse writes inspirational cowboy romance. Her Fair Creek series, set in Indiana, features the Galloway brothers of Galloway Sons Farm. Much like the characters in her stories, Cathy once lived on a farm in "small town" Indiana where she first fell in love with cowboys while visiting the rodeo every summer.

Sign up to receive her newsletter at: www.cathyshouse.com where you'll get free books, exclusive bonus content, and news of her releases and sales.

If you liked this book, please take a moment to review it! Authors (including Cathy) really appreciate this, and it helps draw more readers to books they might like. Thanks!